Every One Still Here

Stories

Liadan Ní Chuinn

GRANTA

Granta Publications, 12 Addison Avenue, London W11 4QR

First published in Great Britain by Granta Books in 2025
This paperback published by Granta Books in 2026
Originally published in Ireland in 2025 by the Stinging Fly Press, Dublin

Copyright © 2025 by Liadan Ní Chuinn

Liadan Ní Chuinn has asserted the moral right to be identified as the author
of this work in accordance with the Copyright, Designs and Patents Act, 1988.

All rights reserved. This book is copyright material and must not be copied,
reproduced, transferred, distributed, leased, licensed or publicly performed or used
in any way except as specifically permitted in writing by the publisher, as allowed
under the terms and conditions under which it was purchased or as strictly permitted by
applicable copyright law. Any unauthorised distribution or use of this text may be a direct
infringement of the author's and publisher's rights, and those responsible may be liable in
law accordingly. Please note that no part of this book may be used or reproduced in
any manner for the purpose of training artificial intelligence technologies or systems.

This collection – with the exception of the final section, 'The Truth', in the final story,
'Daisy Hill' – is a work of fiction, in which all characters and events are fictitious.
Any resemblance to real persons, living or dead, is purely coincidental. 'The Truth'
in 'Daisy Hill' is based on real events and it includes people's real names.

'We All Go' and 'Mary' were first published in *The Stinging Fly*;
'Amalur' was published online by *Granta*.

The quotations from 'Teacht i Méadaíocht'/'Rite of Passage' by Gearóid Mac Lochlainn
are taken from the collection *Sruth Teangacha/Stream of Tongues* by Gearóid Mac Lochlainn,
by kind permission of Cló Iar-Chonnacht. Naomi Shahib Nye, 'No Explosions' from
The Tiny Journalist: copyright © 2019 by Naomi Shihab Nye. Reprinted with the permission
of The Permissions Company, LLC on behalf of BOA Editions, Ltd., boaeditions.org.

A CIP catalogue record for this book is available from the British Library.

3 5 7 9 10 8 6 4 2

ISBN 978 1 80351 329 4 (paperback)
ISBN 978 1 80351 328 7 (ebook)

Set in Palatino
Offset by Iram Allam

Printed and bound by CPI Group (UK) Ltd, Croydon, CR0 4YY

The manufacturer's authorised representative in the EU for
product safety is Authorised Rep Compliance Ltd, 71 Lower Baggot Street,
Dublin D02 P593, Ireland. www.arccompliance.com

www.granta.com

LIADAN NÍ CHUINN was born in the north of Ireland in 1998. *Every One Still Here* is their first book.

'A properly exciting writer . . . One of the most powerful things I've read in recent years' Max Porter

'Stark, unflinching, bald . . . I get the feeling that Ní Chuinn would hate the term "voice of a generation", but it may be foisted on them nonetheless – and with good reason' *Sunday Times*

'Here's a writer who knows how to swerve gracefully from the expected. Their work is instinctive, intriguing and truly exciting' Lisa McInerney

'Ní Chuinn [is] a writer of subtlety despite the polemic that veins these stories . . . Unpredictable and memorable' Chris Power, *Guardian*

'An original, compassionate exploration of grief, faith, forgiveness, heritage and the foundations of shared humanity . . . Never sentimental, the six tales in *Every One Still Here* repeatedly catch readers unawares' *Times Literary Supplement*

'An extraordinary book by an extraordinary author who refuses to look the other way.' Thomas Morris

'There's excitement building around this young writer from the north of Ireland . . . The stories are scrupulous, surprising and entirely gripping. The arrival of a stunning new voice' *Guardian*

'A phenomenal writer, with such a striking, distinctive style. Surreal and yet vivid, wondrous and stark . . . Something new and startling is happening in this work. Fiction is being rejuvenated again' Danny Denton

'For a publisher to agree to publish an anonymous author, as so many did Ferrante, and publishers in Ireland, the UK and the US have Ní Chuinn, that writer has to be extraordinary. And Ní Chuinn is' Rhiannon Lucy Cosslet, *Guardian*

'This is a brilliant and remarkable book . . . Immediately asks to be considered among the island's signal 21st-century literary achievements . . . Superb' Kevin Power, *Irish Times*

'These are exceptional stories . . . Utterly transformative' Neil Hegarty

'An expansive collection of stories set in a present haunted by the past, where history is still happening' *Mslexia*

'Announces Liadan Ní Chuinn as an exciting new voice on the literary scene . . . Outstanding . . . This is a stunning debut' *Irish Independent*

'Phenomenally good . . . Bristles with pain, compassion and controlled fury' *Marie Claire*

'Uncanny and haunting . . . This is literary fiction at its best, and I would recommend *Every One Still Here* to anyone who wants to read something deeply human' *Buzz Magazine*

'Inherited trauma, families, grief and the quiet sorrows of everyday life mark these melancholy, utterly brilliant short stories . . . A remarkable debut' *Irish Daily Mail*

Contents

We All Go	3
Amalur	35
Mary	51
Russia	67
Novena	89
Daisy Hill	115
Acknowledgements	151

Every One Still Here

We All Go

1

My parents were hijacked before I was born. It was just before, two nights prior. I think it's important. I don't know why. They were driving out of the city on a road that got narrow, a bad artery, and then they were stopped in the road by a clot: people with masks and crowbars. My dad was driving so it was my dad who braked.

The people in the road yelled: GET OUT OF THE CAR.

My dad said: Paula. (That was all that he said. He wasn't good at reassurance; when the dog died, he was supposed to break it to us gently, but we said: How is he? and he said: Dead.)

The people with the crowbars yelled: GET OUT OF THE FUCKING CAR.

My dad got out. One of the people took his wallet and checked his ID. (They wanted to be sure they were only hijacking Catholics. His licence said Michael Madigan so they took the car.)

The people with the crowbars yelled: What the fuck is she doing?

My mum hadn't got out. She was very pregnant with me.

The seat belt had locked tight against her, and she couldn't find the belt's plug in the darkness. Her breathing was horrible. She was very scared.

My mum maybe said: Michael, or maybe: I'm stuck. She didn't say anything that could be heard. The men with the masks moved in close. They smashed in the windscreen.

My mum didn't scream but tiny bits of glass bit into her face and her neck. She thought she might never move again but then the seat belt finally gave and she moved like she was melting. My dad took her over to the side of the road. They stood by the hedge where blackberries grow, and badgers bleed out, and the guys with the crowbars drove off in the car. My mum and dad stood in the dark. The night was very cold. It was before mobile phones but my mum wouldn't let them stop at a house to use someone's landline. She was too scared.

I was born two nights later. In the photos I am pink and Michael Madigan is smiling and my mum has those cuts all over her skin, just scabbing, something like co-ordinates/freckles.

It was my dad who told us about the hijacking. He said it was because of tensions at the time: the Orange Order wanted to march through communities that didn't want them. He had determined that this was what it was about because of the hijackers' timing/location/target. My mum's never mentioned it. If it were up to her, we wouldn't know. I only have what my dad told me. (He died when we were starting to be proper people: Bernie was eight and I was twelve.) So I say she was scared, my mum, stuck in the car. I say she thought she might never move again. But I can't know it. She's never told me.

I see that hijacking everywhere. I think it's important. I

don't know why. I feel it in things, as though it's not over. I feel it in the rules that she has. I see it in the way that we live. It's in what she thinks is progressive. She says she wouldn't give us Irish names. She won't let us wear GAA stuff into town. I don't know how to explain it. I see it in her. Bernie talks about the twenty-six counties and the six but my mum, she says Down South, meaning the Republic, meaning the Free State, meaning (depending on where exactly we are) locations at each cardinal point: East, South, North, West. (It bothers us both but Bernie's more straightforward. She says: You're a partitionist, Paula!)

I feel it in the way my mum loves Bernie (fervid, uncomplicated) and the way she sees me (holds me apart).

She has this distance. She says, over the sound of the TV: Jackie, where is it you're away to? She says, she asks me during an ad: Jackie, do you have a girlfriend? and she has to wait for the answer because she really doesn't know / she hasn't noticed / she can't tell.

I don't think that she blames me. That would be stupid. But I wonder about it. I think it's important. If she hadn't been pregnant, she could have got out of the car. The glass wouldn't have cut her. She wouldn't've bled. If she hadn't been pregnant, she wouldn't have been stuck on her own in the dark, watching the men in the masks come closer. She wouldn't have seen Michael Madigan get out of the car and leave her in it. She wouldn't have stood in the cold on bloated, swollen feet. I was in her lap. I was almost born.

I've tried to tell Bernie. She doesn't care. She says: O my fucking god, Jackie. She says: You can't psychoanalyse everything. She says: See if you say this is why you can't pass your driving test—

Bernie doesn't hate me for it, but she wasn't there.

2

We have lectures called Housekeeping. There are lots of rules. It's hard to find the way to the Anatomy Department because the University wants it hidden: people have, in the past, tried to steal bones.

I don't know that I like the people I'm with. I let what they're saying move over me until I can decide. We sit in a clump. There are hundreds of laptops.

The professor has a PowerPoint of photos of different tools/instruments: pincers, surgical scissors, scalpels on a steel tray. The colours are bleached coming through the projector. Each slide has a header with the professor's full name and the long letters of eight qualifications in its wake.

The professor talks about the importance of Anatomy. We are shown sketches from da Vinci's notebook. We are told these are crucial; we are told these are key. (I saw da Vinci's sketches in the museum. They were horrible: he drew travelling people as predators, as thieves. I stood wanting somebody to say it was terrible, the images reproduced on thick paper, framed.) The professor says the most important thing is respect. The professor says that if we miss a session, we'll be disciplined; that this will have serious, potentially devastating, consequences for our careers; that what we will cover in the sessions is vast; that he once had a student expelled for coming to Dissection chewing gum.

This is when I am poked by the person next to me. The girl at the end of our row grins and when each of us have turned, like sunflowers, she blows a pink slabbery bubble.

The others think this is great. I am so embarrassed to be with people who find this funny that I start to sweat. They leave slowly after the lecture, standing together as a group, making plans. I don't want to dislike them so soon (it's Week Two).

I start walking home.

I get in well before Bernie's back from school.

I turn on the TV. I don't care who's talking.

I get bored.

I log on to the Student Portal on the computer. There're videos that're compulsory to watch for the sessions. The professor said admission would be refused to anyone who hadn't seen them, that the Student Portal shares this information. (Bernie would say: A surveillance state.) The folder is called Anatomy. The videos are three minutes each. They've been filmed at an over-the-shoulder angle. There were, I think, maybe only two people involved in their production: the hands with the camera, filming, and the hands with the scalpel. Three people, I think, correcting myself. Three people. The hands will slice into the third person's skin.

The pale hands turn the scalpel round; a voice-over defines and explains certain features. Then the hands and the scalpel move to the flat surface below them, getting closer, as the camera picks up freckles, hair follicles, and the surface is skin; the scalpel slices through skin as though through soap; the scalpel is substituted for pincers to peel back the skin's first thin layer.

I don't mean to lose focus, but the video is slow and unreal. There's glare all over the computer screen, fingerprints and marks from where mum's tried to wipe them.

I check my phone (the first sign of Lack of Respect).

Mum's sent a video into our group chat. She forwards me and Bernie stuff she's been sent on WhatsApp. There's always that warning above: forwarded many times. It's the way chainmail was to me and Bernie when we were small: pictures/animations/stories sent on and on and on. I remember jumpscares, Thinking Of You prayers, badly spelt, long-winded: SEND THIS TO FIFTEEN PEOPLE OR THE KILLER CLOWN WILL BE ABOVE YOUR BED WHEN YOU WAKE.

That was when Michael Madigan died. They're not connected; it was just the same era. Me and Bernie sat at the computer, pushing the back out of the swivel-chair, and my mum sat on the sofa minding Michael Madigan. It happened like that. We sat at that computer, scrapping, and there was, somewhere, some other place in the house, the noise of the shower, the vague sounds of Michael Madigan being washed, the sound of the water and its draining and a slow, chugging extractor fan, the escape from the bathroom of soft wet air, warm and translucent. She brought him back into the TV room, wheeling him carefully. She put on some movie (*Die Hard*/*Live Free or Die Hard*/*A Good Day to Die Hard*) and she closed the blinds and she put down a towel and she cut Michael Madigan's fingernails, while they were soft and surrendering, pushed back cuticles. She made a scrub with coconut oil and thick brown sugar. She put his feet into a basin of warm water (the boke-basin) and she scrubbed, her hand in a pink exfoliating glove, until Michael Madigan's bare legs were matted with rolls of dead skin. She patted his legs dry and coated them with lotion that smelt of factory-flowers. She shaved Michael Madigan's face and she used tiny curved nail scissors to cut the hair out of his ears. Now he'll hear us when we're talking to him. She put a blanket over his knees. They sat on the sofa, at the TV; me and Bernie sat behind, at the computer. I don't know. It's how it happened. There was pain relief. There was infection. There were syringes/alarms/nurses, saying, I've never seen this before. It was, there were, afterwards I knew all these colours: brown as in piss, black as in spit, boke as in yellow, as in blood-red. All these bits. All these speckles. Lumps. There's a spine, bending; shoulders falling down round him. Michael Madigan needed course after course of IV antibiotics and mum thought we were too small to leave at home by ourselves so she drove us all to the hospital and wheeled him in. My mum sat beside him on the sofa in front of us and she told him about this thing Bernie'd said, she was round at a friend's, and they'd been half-watching *Titanic*, and Bernie'd said to this girl's mum, I've a bad feeling about this, as the ship started to sink. It was funny, they'd said. There'd been tears of laughter. Bernie and I heard her. She had Michael Madigan in a towelling dressing-gown, his feet in a pair of disposable slippers. She told him about Bernie. She said it again.

Michael Madigan lost fat from places I didn't even know you had it. When Auntie Shauna finally had her babies, tiny things dressed in pink, everyone said things like, Omygod, aren't they mini, that it seemed so impossible everyone once was that size, that we all could've grown up from something so small. But then, it's how it happened, then Michael Madigan was so thin that it made perfect sense. He could have been folded, packed up, made the same size as those children: premature, unready.

Flesh melted off Michael Madigan's wrists and hands and fingers until his wedding band couldn't even stay on his finger. It's another infection, said the nurse. This is dangerous. It's all dangerous. But there was nothing to do. Michael Madigan couldn't speak. Nobody could help. My mum was there, all the time, minding him. She stroked his face.

Jackie, says Bernie.

She makes me jump.

You left the front door open, she says. Not wide open, but like. Still.

I log out of the computer.

She goes to the kitchen and puts the toaster on. She stands against the counter on her phone, waiting.

I say, Do you remember Ash?

She doesn't want to look up, but in the end, she says, sighing, The dog?

She says, Is that why you look like that?

There are big stretches between her sentences.

I say, I was thinking about dad.

Bernie says, About Michael?

Bernie says, Why?

She puts spread on the toast. She only eats Flora. She says, Are you in again tomorrow?

Yeah. 9 to 4.

Gross.

She lays down on the sofa and eats her toast. She looks sorry for herself, that she's had to come home to this (me). She looks at her phone. She doesn't get up.

My mum gets in later. She's not in bad form. She says, I could eat a horse, which means she'll eat toast, and she says, It looks like a bomb's gone off in here, Jack, looking at my bag on the table and my boots on the floor. She sits on the sofa and crunches on toast. She says, Bernie, love, any biz?

Bernie starts something about teachers. She builds to a punchline and my mum cackles.

When there's a pause, I say, See this weekend, I'm going up to see Auntie Shauna.

The atmosphere changes so fast it feels physical.

Bernie says, Why?

My mum stands up. She brushes crumbs from her workclothes. She says, Well, Jackie, you're a big boy now. Knock yourself out.

I don't want to upset her. It's just how it happens.

She goes upstairs.

Bernie's looking at me like I'm a freak.

I snap: What?

She says, What are you doing?

But she doesn't want an answer, she's only answering me.

We listen to the sound of our mum on the stairs, her step firm. The stairs in this house are so steep that they're dangerous. She fell down the stairs when they first moved in here, down a whole flight, and she broke her ribs. Ribs can't be set like another fracture. Even now, sometimes, she'll groan when she's moving.

When Michael got sick, he couldn't even try the stairs. He was grounded, like the dog used to be. My mum got him a bed by the sofa, and I think she had to sleep down here with him. I'm not sure. I don't think I remember it all.

When we were little, she used to say she could feel something on the landing: a presence, a person who used to live here. She said they were friendly and we shouldn't be scared. I never felt it. Bernie said she did, but she just meant she was afraid. Nobody said it again after my dad died. Ghosts are only interesting if you haven't any yourself.

*

3

We've been emailed our group allocations. I will be in the second group.

At the lockers, there is fuss. We need a workbook for the session. We need change for the locker. As we put on coats and IDs, the first group comes out through the big double doors just ahead of us. I see the girl who blew gum at the end of the row. She says to me, going past, It's really good! and she smiles with teeth that are visibly wet.

There's a graduate who checks our IDs at the door, who scans us in with a barcode reader, who says, grab a seat at a work-station, as we pass, and people take stools at the work-stations, we all take stools at the work-stations, as though the work-station is not a bench on which lies a yellowed chunk of person. A lad I know from lectures takes the stool next to me. He says, y'alrightJackie, all one word. He's almost my height.

Our bench has a laminated label: STATION 8, and questions, printed out and laminated, by its side: kidneys/their survival; sympathetic/parasympathetic nervous supply; blood vessels, lymph, their sources and drainage? Our bench has somebody's entire abdomen. It's dry/embedded with silicon. It's old, so some of it is coming off in plasticated flakes. It smells. Whatdyouthink? my partner says, putting his face down close. Whatdyousay for this one, Renal Artery? Yeah?

STATION 6 is someone's leg, cut off at the thigh and running down to their shin.

STATION 11 has questions about salivary glands. It has somebody's head. One half of the face, split down a vertical line, is hollowed out, to show the glands, but the other half is just normal, just a cold waxy face: a scrunched-up nose, an eyebrow, eyelashes, nose hair in the nostrils, their naked scalp from a head shaved.

My partner picks them up. He holds their head in his hand.

I have my stomach pushed tight against the table. I breathe through my mouth.

He asks me a question.

I don't know.

He is asked a question.

Nobody knows anything.

We were told, in the series of lectures called Anatomy Department: Housekeeping, that every body in the department was given as a gift. People knew about the university's work. They thought about it. They chose us. I know this. I know what the professor said. I press my stomach hard against the table. But did they know they weren't going to stay whole? But did they sign that their head could be taken off at the neck? These are ovaries. This is a torso. This is someone's penis, pubic hair still intact. Here are limbs and digits, yellow and flaking. Did they know they'd be split over benches with laminated pages and questions? What if they thought that their gift would cure cancer?

I mean, they can't tell me. They just lay there. People my age (hungover/flirting) lean over them, try to answer questions they don't understand.

The time drags on. People start to leave early.

There's a girl snapping bones together. Her partner asks a question and she says brightly: I'm just playing!

The lad from lectures asks me if I want to get lunch when this is over. I say, No.

4

I know things, but not the people. This is all I know, facts one-line long: my dad's dad Jackie and his older brother Ciarán were interned. Jackie died seven years later. Ciarán managed eleven. I've looked online so I've read some of the things the British Army did to the hundreds of civilians they took away and held captive, held without charge: water-boarding, injections, electric shocks, mock-executions, starvation, sleep-deprivation, sensory-deprivation, harassment by dogs, dragging people behind vehicles.

I don't know that all of these things happened to Jackie and Ciarán, but I know they were interned and then they were never the same. I know that they died (seven/eleven years later).

I don't know what these things did to Michael Madigan.

This is my family: Ciarán was one year older than Kate, who was two years older than Michael, who was four years older than Shauna. So when British soldiers came through the door and dragged out my dad's dad and my dad's brother Ciarán, my dad was fifteen and his sister Shauna was eleven and his sister Kate was seventeen (but she emigrated, so what's she to us now?).

I know that Ciarán died in his twenties.

Their dad died before, when they were all still so young (though not as young as me and Bernie were when Michael Madigan died). Their dad died seven years after the raid/internment. Shauna was still in school. My dad was in Belfast, at the Tech. When Jackie died, Kate went to America and never came back.

This is all I know.

I send Shauna a message on WhatsApp. She still lives near where they grew up, and it's she has the farm and what's left of its house. Her husband has cattle on some of the fields that are turning to rushes.

She messages back pretty fast. She says: O hello my gorgeous nephew! it wld be brill to see you & Bernadette! though I didn't mention Bernie.

She says I can go, so I'll go.

Bernie comes up to my room. It's late. She lies down on the bed as though it is hers.

I messaged Shauna, I say.

So you're going, she says. She rolls over so her back is to me.

You can come if you want.

Yeah, she says. I know.

Sounds come out her phone. There are people shrieking on Instagram stories and noises from dances/TikToks/reaction videos. Then she puts the phone down, and it all goes quiet. The room's dark. Her breathing sounds vaguely asthmatic.

She's asleep.

I don't move her. The room's cold; she'll wake when she feels it.

I listen to the sound of her. It's so familiar. We shared a room for a stupidly long time because mum didn't want to change the house round again; there were still—the house had places—things were where Michael Madigan had left them.

Bernie snores. She always talked in her sleep. Sometimes she said my name and I woke. Sometimes she spoke and she spoke and I only woke when she stopped.

Once mum found her out on the landing with her eyes

wide open. My mum said, Bernie, love, what are you doing? and Bernie said: Who are you? Why am I here?

My mum said the normal things said to someone sleepwalking: Come on, let's go, you're dreaming, back to bed, but Bernie was angry and stressed and upset.

Mum had her hands. She tugged her back to our room. She said, Jackie, don't get up. She pulled Bernie onto her bed. She lay down beside her. I could see them in the corridor-light, my mum rubbing Bernie's back. She said, bird, you're alright. Bernie sounded like she was crying. She said, I don't understand. My mum lay there. I don't remember her leaving.

5

Today is the first day that we have Dissection. The previous session was Prosection: all of the cutting was done for us. I see the same group at the lockers. It's 8.47am.

I focus very hard on buttoning my coat. I hold my ID card at the correct angle for the technician's barcode scanner. I pull on the gloves. There is this shuffle of us moving slowly forward. I watch my shoes under the white coat, watch the stranger in front of me, and I do it carefully, I do it with all of my focus, but still when it's done, I have to go into the room, and the chill of it makes me sad and afraid.

The room is huge. It has a very high ceiling, like a vault. It's cold as a fridge. In front of us, in rows, are stainless steel tables on wheels, each one holding up a shape covered with plastic sheeting. It looks like a morgue/a nightmare and it smells like a butcher's but with chemicals mixed in. The professor is here, though not for long; there are excuses given. The professor will start us off, and then my cohort will be under the guidance, the care, of the technician. The professor says, if you feel strange, you can leave. Is that clear? Just go. I realise that this is but the first of these sessions.

I feel strange. I feel the numbness of it, about to do something I can never undo.

The technician says, Everyone find a table.

People start to move themselves over to the stations, start to clump themselves at the masked/hidden outlines.

The technician says, Groups of no more than 5.

I go with the same crowd. We stand in the far corner. I do it only because it's easy, only because already there is the feeling of having missed something crucial, of everyone knowing each other from another place, from before. Two more come over. The new lads have their ID cards stuck to the breast-pocket of their white lab coats, visible. They've photos of themselves from Sixth Form for their picture.

I should feel more than I do. I want to bite my nails but we're all wearing these thick blue gloves. I think of the video I watched, of fingers holding scalpels.

The professor says: Everyone, pull back the covers.

The intention is demonstrated at the professor's nearest table. The covers are taken back, three layers of different plastics, until we see a naked body with the top half of its head completely gone, that is: with none of its brain or the skull that held it.

The lad I know from lectures pulls back our covers.

There is a dead naked woman with half a head.

The professor says something to the technician. They say hushed, unhurried things to each other and at first there is silence, there is only our breathing, but then the people at the bodies start talking to each other, too. In this corner, one guy says to the others, so what school did youse go to?

The professor leaves. The technician takes a central position.

Okay, the technician says. Everyone relax.

The technician says, Slowly, now, just whenever you're ready, I want you to touch your body, pressing the blue glove of their hand against the skin of the closest body.

The boys with the Sixth Form ID photos look at each other. I know that they're going to touch our woman first. They press on her forearm (first gently, then hard) and they kind of laugh. The other lad touches the woman's shoulder. He rubs the pads of his gloved fingers on her skin. He says, does this remind anyone else of Granny In The Graveyard? The laughter is quick, hard.

They're not looking at me but I know that they know I don't want to do it. I push my finger against the woman's upper arm. Even through the thick blue glove, it feels rigid and unfamiliar, her skin like leather from being embalmed.

I drop my hand.

At the central table, there is the technician, cutting into a man's skin, peeling away layers, working down into his adipose tissue. The technician is talking about scalpels, and people at the central table bend their necks in round the body. They want to see everything. Already people are like that: they need to be ahead.

The technician picks up a large metal bowl, stainless steel exactly like the table, and says, This is very important! Is everyone listening? Everything you take from your body must go into the bowl at the end of your table. Have a look! Every table has one, you see? You must put everything from your body into your body's bowl because the contents of these bowls get returned with the person to their family. It is absolutely critical that all their tissue is kept together and not mixed up.

Then the technician places skin in that body's bowl, drops

in white fascia and curds of yellow fat.

One of the lads' stomach rumbles and the rest of them piss themselves.

I look at our woman. She only has half a face but there's enough left to see her nose, which is broken, bent to one side from the weight of her body lying down on itself for however many months it was before she was ready.

One of the boys says, I've heard all the fluid gathers in certain places. Like wherever there's fat gathered, it completely liquefies in the embalming, so when you cut in all the fat and formaldehyde is just liquid together. You cut in and it hits you with splashback. Swear to god. My brother's in fourth year, he says, it hit him in the eyes.

That's all for today.

The technician watches us go.

6

The dog died two years before Michael Madigan. He picked us up from primary school the day after the night mum'd rushed her to the vet's. The dog was called Ash. He was huge and kind (a rescue greyhound).

Bernie and I were in the back of the car, strapped into our seats, looking at each other. We were quiet/waiting to hear when he was coming home. He had to tell us sometime.

But he didn't.

In the end we said, at once, over each other: Where's Ash? Is he sick? Is he home?

Michael Madigan said: He's dead.

He didn't say anything else. Maybe once, Awk, Bernie, because Bernie was crying (she was howling with grief). He drove. We got home. Mum came out to the car and she picked Bernie up (even though she was, like, six).

He said, He's dead, but not to be mean, or cruel. He said it pretty softly, and only because it was true.

When we were those ages, six and ten, Bernie still had a booster-seat, and she sat directly behind him, but I was the other side, so I could see him at a diagonal. I could see some of his face across the way, and I remember how he looked in ways that maybe she doesn't (dark beard, light skin, freckles, the arm of his jumper, rolled up at the wrist; bitten nails, freckled hands).

I remember him in ways that she can't.

He steers with one hand, keeps both off when he can. When there's sun for a second, he winds his window all the way down and sits with his whole arm out of the car. He drives as though it is the simplest thing in the world. He drives as though he could just as well be dreaming. If someone cuts him off or won't let him out or we're stuck in traffic coming home from school, he doesn't care. He turns his CD on. His favourite band in the world is Simple Minds. His favourite album is *Street Fighting Years* and he plays it, non-stop, from 1 to 11. It's not his favourite, but he doesn't mind 'Belfast Child'. He drums his fingers on the steering wheel, he moves his head but it's all, always, so out of time. He speaks the words along to the singing.

I didn't know he was going to die. Nobody did.

He drives and Bernie's loud in the back of the car. I call him Michael Madigan as though that makes him Not My Dad. I'm sorry about it, but it puts distance between us.

He nods along, erratically, to music that's never-ending, to Track 11 as it becomes Track 1, over and over, again and again, driving us home and home and home.

7

I can't stop thinking about Anatomy. There are dozens of faces there, cold, like at a wake, turned to face me from their tables and I am supposed to say: I can identify the submandibular gland, poke and point, as though that is normal and healthy and good.

I look at my hands and I see Michael Madigan's. Freckles, chewed nails. His hands, turned over, had palms of calloused skin. He used to have a wedding band, before it wouldn't fit him anymore.

It's Friday. Bernie goes into school but I don't get up. I have some lectures but I'm not going in. This week coming, on the days we don't have lectures, we will cut into a person, peel back their skin and work down to the fat (adipose tissue). I think of the rooms (fridges), all their fragmented wakes. I'm scared that I'll do it. I'm scared that I won't mind.

Bernie gets home at four but she doesn't come find me.

When my mum gets in, I hear the hum of them talking, and then my mum comes up the stairs. She takes them even slower than usual. She opens my door and stands at it awkwardly. She says, Bernie said you were up here. I think: she should have had only daughters. She doesn't know what to do with me. I think it. I almost say it.

My mum says, Have you gotten up today?

I don't answer.

She says, How're you doing, anyway? Bernie tells me she's worried about you.

There are long pauses when we speak to each other, like a time delay as we reach each other's continents or the time-lag needed to run messages through translators.

I say, It's gross, I guess. It's heavy. All these bodies and heads and you're not allowed to be bothered.

My mum says, Jesus Christ, Jackie. Is that it? It's your course? You don't like it, she says, shrugs. Well, it was your bloody choice.

I go downstairs later to make beans on toast. She and Bernie are watching a DVD on Bernie's laptop, each with one half a pair of white earphones. It looks like *Princess And The Frog* on the screen. Bernie's kind of a baby like that.

My mum said once that it was my dad's idea to call her Bernadette. They called me Jackie after his dad, but it was she thought of that; when Bernie was born, it was Michael Madigan had all the ideas. He really liked Bernadette. He couldn't even explain why.

There are things about the saint that Bernie found out on Wikipedia: she didn't know any French until she was 13; she spoke Occitan (Bernie said, A Minority Language Queen). But we don't believe Michael Madigan meant the saint at all. He meant Bernadette McAliskey. Bernie read her book as a PDF that she found online—we were born into an unjust system; we are not prepared to grow old in it—she wrote things like that. She was huge in the Civil Rights Movement here. She was imperative, says Bernie. She was key.

These Bernies are part of how she sees herself. I think they're important. She holds them, palms outstretched, like the icons of Jesus have him carry holes in his hands.

They make her who she is.

She's good, in this way that I'm not. It's there, in the difference between us. It's like when Michael Madigan's things got destroyed with the damp. We didn't know until we started to clear out his study so me and Bernie wouldn't be in the one room anymore. We didn't know until mum pulled this box down from a shelf and opened it and his things, the files, were wet with damp, and fuzzed with mould, and then it was, I knew, we felt, we had been doing it just for so long then, trying not to notice, the house getting weaker and worse with no Michael Madigan to fix it, bulbs blown and not replaced, blinds broken, the TV room window jammed shut, unopened. It was Bernie who held my mum then, through the crying. It was Bernie made her drink fluids. She was curled up in a ball, and Bernie was saying, I am so, so sorry, and I could hear her, but I couldn't say it. I don't know why. I checked the front and back doors were locked. I closed the curtains in every room. I could hear them. The fabric of my mum's top made a sound when Bernie rubbed her back.

We cleared out his study, finally, after that. It took a long time. I sleep there now. All I have, I remember, I was twelve when he died and before that, these final things, I remember Michael Madigan's nails trimmed right down, his hands so still and they couldn't grip, the sound of a fan oven working up to heat, me and Bernie sat eating food from the tray, his eyes (watering, bloodshot, scared), she hummed when she rubbed the medicated cream into his cracked skin, working carefully, calmly, until it was covered. Michael, she said, Michael, don't you worry. She left a hot water bottle up for us, every night, in me and Bernie's beds. The radio was on. We lay beside him so close we could all feel the movements of each other breathing. It couldn't be stopped once it had started. It spread. It ran all through him.

At first, it looked like there wasn't much wrong, and there wasn't really, except that his hands shook and sometimes he fell going down the steep stairs. That was what he went to the GP about. He thought he'd need meds/maybe glasses. But then he was sick, not well at all, forcing himself upright to sit straight in the chair, loose pyjama shirts, ribs running down his corrugated chest, trying to make the nurses laugh, having to listen to someone talk about medication and miming shooting himself with his fingers, but then his body was just like a doll's, lax and unmoving. No weight, no fat. Bones. Joints. He looked at things but he didn't see them. There were things that couldn't be proven without his input, so it was like: is he blind? Can he hear us? It was the end, but I didn't know it was the end. If I hold his hand and I squeeze it until it's warm, can he feel that? Does he exist in his body anymore?

My mum told us that he did. My mum told us that he was thinking things about himself and about us, saying into himself, I love you, when we told him good night.

But I know that at night I lay there, hearing Bernie breathe beside me, thinking that if he didn't know what was happening, his thoughts could only be like her sleep-talking: full of questions/fear.

At night, I think: if he knew what was happening, isn't that worse?

8

Bernie's eyes are puffy when she's just woken up. She groans. But she gets out of bed because she's coming with me. We walk into town and then get the bus from the centre. It's going to take an hour and a half going out. I text Shauna, and she meets us at the bus stop when we get into the town. She's made her daughters get out of the car so they're stood beside her, cringing. Girls, Shauna says, these are your cousins! and she beams at us as though none of us have ever met.

Wow! says Bernie. You're so big!

Nine, says Shauna, like it's a miracle.

We have met them before, but we don't see them often. They have names like a perfume. They were three when Michael died. They don't remember. We get into her car and she drives us home.

Her house is rural and new. It's big in that way which is kind of needless, with tarmac on the driveway and a tap with water that comes out boiling. But Shauna is nice. She talks a lot. She calls Bernie 'Bernadette'. She says, What'll youse have to eat? Some toast? Butter? God, it's awful early. She talks so much that it starts to move over me, and Bernie shoves me because I'm not answering questions.

Did you want to see the farm, Jackie? Shauna repeats. She's very nice.

I say, Yeah.

She nods. You'll enjoy seeing round it again, I'm sure.

Shauna's husband gets in. Shauna says he's been golfing. He smiles, but he doesn't bother making small talk (things like saying: Hello). Shauna asks if he's free to babysit The Girls and he hesitates.

When she's finally let go, she drives me and Bernie. Bernie sits in the front, which makes Shauna laugh for some reason, and I sit behind her, looking at Shauna through the diagonal. It's so hard to believe that she's as related to our dad as Bernie is to me, that she could have known him like that. She talks a lot, even when she's driving. We pass new-build houses that she says were never there before. A house in every field now, she says, in a tone like she doesn't herself live in a new-build sat in an old field.

It's been so long since we've been up here that I don't see it coming and the turn-off is sudden. Shauna parks up on grass and says, We'll walk on up.

She waits for me and Bernie to get out of the car, talks about bugs on her windscreen, about how there are barely any now. Used to be in September your screen would be smoky with them, she says. But I guess you guys don't remember that.

Bernie shakes her head.

Shauna sighs. I see it on the TV. There's concern, you know. When the bugs go, we all go. That's what they say.

We follow her up the hill. Me and Bernie aren't in the right shoes. Shauna points at her husband's cattle in the next field over. She says that this used to be meadow, but the land is all rushes now and she doesn't know why.

We keep walking. There are two bent-over trees with no leaves, and two falling down out-buildings, and then what's left of the house. From this distance, it looks like the roof is green, but then we get closer and it's lichen/moss/rotting roof tiles.

It's a bungalow. The windows are smashed and the front door is broke open. I go up to the door. The hall takes a sharp right. There's a Sacred Heart of Jesus looking back at me, an old red lamp beneath it that used to glow red.

The wind is fairly loud and brutal. It's cold.

Bernie talks to Shauna, and I can hear in her tone that she's angry with me. She's uncomfortable, pretending not to be, and she's blaming me for it. She asks Shauna about the house. She says, Was this not quite small for all of you?

Shauna says, O god, yeah. Of course. Sure, all of us children were in one room for the longest time, and then when we were too grown for that, me and Kate were put in with our parents. It was always two to a bed. And people stayed, you know, cousins. People came out for the summer because it was safer than the towns. It's mad to think.

They talk about small things. Bernie wants to know when they got a TV, and did they know their neighbours. I wait until it seems like there is no time left and then I say it, I say: When they were interned, Jackie and Ciarán—

Shauna says, immediately, so that it comes out at almost the same time and I know then that the whole time she's been braced, she's been waiting: I don't remember, love. Honestly, Jackie, I don't.

Bernie's staring at me. It's so cold. Nobody says anything.

I'm very loud inside my own head. I think of people (innocent) dragged out of houses, apartments, red-brick terraces, driven away down these old lanes to internment camps. People here paying money in taxes for the Army which came for them. I have their names in my head— Jackie, Ciarán, Michael—I want to meet them. I need to see them. This is my family. This is my dad's dad, and my dad's brother, and my dad. I can feel the blood in my head. This is home, isn't it? This is where we all come from. So why aren't they here? Why's there nobody here?

Shauna says, There was one night when we were in the car and your dad was driving. It was after he'd gone to the Tech but he was up for the weekend. It was me, Kate, your dad, and a friend of mine. We got stopped at a checkpoint and they made him get out. It was raining. It was almost dark. The soldiers had guns. They made him strip.

Shauna says, We were in the car. We couldn't do anything. It was like that. None of us said a word. I don't know how long he was out there. I was crying, and Kate was furious with me for it. He got back in. He was soaked through. He drove us home.

Bernie says, my mum told me about, like, a night raid? Her voice is high and uneasy. They came in and they took your dad and you were crying, or something, and your mum was screaming but they wouldn't let her go to you.

Shauna says, They think they're brave.

She says, They do it to mess with your head. She says, And doesn't it work?

Which is as close to what happened to Ciarán as she's willing to get.

I stand very still. The wind is angry. There's nobody left who can answer my questions. So how can I tell them that I still feel it? They're here, inside me, clots, lumps, valves in my heart that never quite close, things unspoken as though that makes them unseen. I look at the house (horrible windows, broken door) and I see British soldiers. I look at that Jesus (I hear prayers/I see lights).

Bernie is saying, And have you read about what the Brits did in Kenya? You cannot imagine it. You literally can't. She stops kind of awkwardly. She says, Jackie, what's wrong?

Shauna says, O, Jackie. O, Jackie, love. She comes over to hug me but she can't reach very high. I think Bernie will say something (Gross!) but she doesn't.

Shauna says: It's hard, pet. I know it is.

She's so nice.

It's sad seeing it like this, she says.

I say, Yeah.

I don't know what I expected.

Something came for him, took him, ate him up. Does it live here? Did it follow him into the city? Why am I thinking about him? It's all like this: wasted, rotted, reedy, broke.

There can be nothing rewound or undone.

Shauna says, You'll stay for a good lunch, at least. It's cold up here, you know. She says quietly, like someone other than us might hear her: It's a bit morbid.

9

When he was driving us places, he'd make us spell random words. He'd say Combine Harvester or Industrial Estate or Pedestrian. Bernie was shit at it but then she was always younger than me.

I had a teacher at primary school who told us that we had to love God more than our families. I took it to heart; that is, it worried me. I asked Michael Madigan if he loved God, and he hesitated.

I want to know more than anybody can tell me. Was he happy? Was he content? Was he satisfied with his life when it started ending? Was he angry? Was he angry about Jackie, and Ciarán, and internment, the night the soldiers stripped him with his sisters in the car, the night they broke in, every night there's ever been when things were horrible and wrong? Who was he? Who does that make me?

Did he miss me?

He had a beard and freckles and big dark eyebrows. His hands and his arms were not pale at all. When he got sick, mum kept his face shaved. He didn't look anything like himself.

Did he know how fucking shit this would be, with him being dead forever and ever, there never being a day of its easing, never one hour when I can see him again, when he can just sit on the sofa and do my head in and for once in my life, I can breathe?

I said I was thinking of him and Bernie said, Why?

I remember more than her, but that just makes it lonely.

He wasn't old. Even now, he's not old.

There was a day when Shauna came up to see him. She didn't bring her husband and she didn't bring the Girls. It was near the end, but I didn't know that then.

Shauna was very nice. She said, Paula, I've just been listening to this beautiful radio programme in the car. I could only think of you. Let me stick it on for a minute, you'll know exactly what I mean. My mum got her little portable radio. Shauna fussed with the stations until she reached one playing 'Bí Thusa Mo Shúile'. It was that kind of programme: Catholic choral music, songs that'd be sung by a part-time choir at Mass. It brings me right back, said Shauna, her eyes wide. God, doesn't it just take you right back? Then Shauna said, Here, I'll give it to Michael.

My mum said, Well. She hesitated. She said, He's still in bed. She said, Okay. Sure, we'll let him have a listen. She turned up the volume and brought the radio over to my dad.

I said, He's going to hate it. He loves Simple Minds.

Jesus, Jackie, my mum said. He's such a Debbie Downer, she said to Shauna. She left the radio in beside my dad and came back to Shauna, stood at the counter in the kitchen. She'd made us all tea. Shauna talked about their new car. She talked about her husband. She talked about the farm: her husband'd spotted some reeds in one field; he didn't know where they were from. I've been racking my brains, said Shauna. But there just never were any reeds there before. She talked about the Girls. They were still very little, but growing in accordance with what the GP expected. Mum asked if Shauna would eat a few Birds Eye potato waffles and Shauna said she wouldn't say no, Paula, she wouldn't say no! My mum leant across to stick the oven on. There was the hum of it.

By the time I remembered about Shauna's music playing at my dad's head, he'd been listening to the choral programme for forty minutes. It'd've had him tortured. He would have been spitting. He hates that kind of music. He would have been saying, For fuck sake, Shauna, you call that music! He would have been saying, I'll show you music, taking out a CD, insisting on listening to one album, right through.

Bernie started laughing and that set me off. He'd listened to this stupid fucking choral music for forty minutes, we were pissing ourselves, Shauna was hands-at-her-mouth laughing, the radio still playing.

But that was only how it started, because it turned out, actually, that it was one of those things that is funny at first but then you accidentally think about it too much and it's horrific, it is so sad that it could make you vomit just to think about, it is literally horrible, so horribly sad.

I don't even know how to forgive us for that.

10

In the car on the drive back to Shauna's house and her Girls, Bernie sits in the front and they talk about Bernie's friends. Bernie tells Shauna the kind of stories, rising to crescendo, that mum loves to hear and Shauna says, Bernadette Madigan, you are only hilarious.

It makes me think about my mum and Bernie, the way that they fit together. They're like those ornaments made in two parts: you can take Bernie away, and Bernie's still whole, but taking her away leaves my mum with this crater, this shape down her side where Bernie should be. I lean my head against the car window and I let my head move with the hum of the glass. I think I can see bog cotton up on the hills, like the fine fair hairs that cover a face, waving tails of it. Bernie always says to my mum, You're a partitionist, Paula! I don't believe in a British border! But what, I think, what if the others do? Because it's been like this, for years on years on years. It's like, nothing's real when it's happening in the north. It's only real pain when it happens to other people. It only matters when somebody else is dead, and then they start peace-groups, and then they write songs saying that it's in our head, and they sing that, and they say that, as though none of it happened. They still believe they're Irish and we're not because the Brits tell them so. (Bernie says they never freed Ireland, they just changed the definition of her.)

I'm not even saying that I can't understand it. I know it'd be simpler to ignore when the British Army ran our children over, shot them dead. I'm not stupid.

When the nurses came to see Michael Madigan, I hated it. Bernie sat on mum's lap, and how was that fair? They had each other. It was alright for them, when they could wrap around each other like a Celtic knot.

When the hospice people came, I said I was sick. I said I had diarrhoea if I had to. Mum wanted me and Bernie to speak to the staff on our own so that we could say anything that was on our minds, but Bernie had this way (I think she's forgotten) of saying all in one gulp: When is he going to die? in the exact tone she said, What's your name? Are you a nurse? (She was seven, eight years old.)

I didn't want to be there. I didn't want to know anything. I didn't want to sit on the sofa while Bernie asked when my dad would die and the nurse gave her a sticker or a sweet or held her hand (I don't know, I never went).

There was a peace that I knew when I had Michael Madigan. There was a warmth in the world when I had a dad. Sometimes I feel it so strongly: nothing that happened can actually have happened. There'll be a day when I look over and it'll all be undone.

Shauna waits with us at the bus stop. She says loud things to Bernie about school, and AS levels (they've bonded). People think they owe nobody, that they owe nothing. And I don't know why they don't care. I know that I'd care. All I see is her hands, the way she looked after Michael Madigan. All I see's it all together, tied like a knot.

Jackie, you're awful like him, Shauna says. You know, like *The Quiet Man*.

11

He's driving me back from an eighth birthday party. It's only me and him in the car. He says, well, Jackie-boy. Let's see if you can pass this test.

I'm excited/kind of nervous.

He turns down the music so I can hear him clearly.

If someone came up to you and said, excuse me, sir, I'd like to buy your dog. Here is one hundred pounds. What would you say?

No!

You wouldn't sell Ash?

He's driving, and talking, and it's all for me.

Good, he says. What about if someone wasn't asking for money, they just really, really wanted him, needed him even, what'd you say then?

I don't say anything.

You don't know?

I don't think so.

Need more context? he says. That's good, too.

He stops looking ahead. He looks at a diagonal, straight into me.

What're you doing, fucking about with that Anatomy stuff? he says. You're not doing it for me, kid. You know I don't care.

I don't say anything.

The people are weird, he says.

Yeah. Maybe.

Are you happy? he says. Are you content?

Michael Madigan reaches his arm out and pokes me. Jackie, he says, you don't even remember what I sound like. You're guessing.

I say, So?

I say, That's not my fault. You didn't lose your voice all at once. It was so slow, we all kept adapting. I don't remember what you sounded like at the start, but it's like mum says, boiling frogs. None of us do.

He says, I would never speak this much.

I look at him. I watch his hands on the steering wheel. Da, I say, I wish you'd tell me something.

Michael Madigan yells, Get out of the car, Paula! and falling glass hits us with the burn of acid rain.

Amalur

Berezi's husband hit their dog and my boyfriend said after, I hate it when he does that. He was very upset. I knew as soon as the man hit the dog that I hated him and that this act was terrible, but the circumstances were such that I didn't say anything. My boyfriend and I were out at the lake. This man was Berezi's husband: he was married to my boyfriend's older sister.

We were all at the lake and in fact walking in opposite directions around it. My boyfriend saw the man first and he waved. The man stopped when he was close to us because he felt he had to. The dog he had with him barked at my boyfriend (he was wearing a hat) and then the man (Berezi's husband) hit the dog until it stopped. Then the man was breathless. His cheeks were red.

That he was married to my boyfriend's sister seemed impossible to believe. Almost any time I saw her, I wanted to scream about how horrible her husband was. How couldn't she see it? What was she thinking? There are billions of men in this world, the world is literally covered in them, but this man, this man—the circumstances were such that I kept it together.

Despite it all, I didn't say anything.

I liked my boyfriend's family. His parents, that is, his mother and father, were Basque. He had a step-mother, who was nice. He had this step-mother because his mother had died, long enough ago that there was little trace of her left in the house or in their conversation. There was little trace of her except that once when Aitor was tidying the living room, he rolled up the rug, and there was a circle of blood staining its underside, and he explained that when his wife was dying, all her hair had fallen out, so her head had been covered with nothing but bare skin, unprotected, and she had fallen trying to get out of her seat, and her head was cut open with the force of the fall, and though he had gotten the blood out of the rug's actual fibres, he had never managed to shift the stain underneath. There was no trace of her except that she was there in my boyfriend, in his sisters, in his older brother—after many years, I found her as a scientist finds a black hole: there she was, in the absence; there she was, at the centre. She was the reason they moved as they did.

At the time I am thinking of, my boyfriend's family was like this: his older brother was long ago lost to America; his older sister, Berezi, was married but often around; his little sister, Lur, was fourteen, small for her age; his step-mother and father were comfortable, amiable, I would say; he and I were twenty, at the College but both still living at home.

We spent a lot of time at his house because it was a nice place to be. His family had dinners like I hadn't believed anyone did: if it was dark, they lit candles; if it was bright, they ate outside; they arranged plates with serving spoons and passed around bread. They liked to sit on chairs on the deck outside afterwards. They liked to say ecstatic things about the moon. It was very calming.

I'm not saying my boyfriend or his family took it for granted, but I don't think they knew how rare it was for families to be calming, to pass bread around. When he and I had been going out for a long time, Berezi told me that I should bring round my mother, because of how long we had been going out. You're here all the time and we know you so well—this is what they said—we should have met her already! It's no trouble at all!

In truth, I asked my mother only in the confidence that she would refuse. I texted. I said: *You don't want to have dinner with my boyfriend's family do you?* I worded the message carefully, so that it would be as easy as possible for her to answer: *No*. I did this consciously; the message had three drafts. She replied some twenty minutes later. *Let me know what day*, she typed, *ill take the evening off work*.

So I brought her.

It hurt me that she came, it hurt that she would do this for me. She sat at the table, flinching, twisting with the effort. She went to the bathroom three times. She hesitated when passed dishes, as though she feared any moment someone might say, put that down, how dare you take that! She did not know what to do with the dishes so that, gradually, people stopped—the meal was unmoving.

They tried to make conversation. It jolted. It jerked. She spoke when my boyfriend's father, Aitor, asked her something, asked her something to which the answer was a story about, as a child, finding an almost dead hare, and running for neighbours who rang a vet who said they could only kill it, and finding the neighbours refused to help her, and how she stood, crying, looking at this struggling little life, trying to decide if she was brave enough to do what would end its pain.

The silence was terrible when my mother finished speaking. She was close to tears and her hand kept rising to her throat as though she were close to vomiting.

The evening never recovered.

My mother was mortified. She is not oblivious. Lur cleared the table and we sat on chairs on the decking outside. My mother kept trying to leave, but as a charitable gesture, Berezi was obviously not going to let her go until she and my mother had had a normal exchange.

I knew Berezi. I was sure this was so that when my mother and I were away from this family, I could repeat this one normal exchange, assure ourselves that everything had been fine, that we had all done fine.

But my mother was desperate to leave. Her skin was a strange grey. She and I never ate together. Her hands kept moving to her throat, to her face. We didn't have mealtimes, or conversations. It was a sustained charitable effort on Berezi's part. I could see my mother, reaching beyond the absolute end of her limits. Having tried perhaps half a dozen topics, Berezi was asking about the Basque language. One of their mother's parents was monolingual, had only Euskara, she was saying. My mother seemed barely conscious within her grey skin. The baby, Berezi was saying, is Ihintza.

Berezi's husband came out onto the deck, car keys swinging. Their stepmother started to say something welcoming, but the man spoke over her. Time to go, he said.

It seemed to me that he noticed, then, Berezi's enthusiasm. Go on, her husband said, in such a way that we knew she should not. You're a broken fucking record, Berezi, he said. I thought he pronounced her name wrong. I tried not to hear him. I sat like my mother, twitching. I moved like their dog had, when he had come in: I flinched, I tried to move away. Berezi stood. They left.

I walked my mother home, with nothing comforting to tell her. At ours, she vomited in the kitchen sink when we got inside. She was so stressed I believe that she blacked-out, that no memories formed, because after that night when I mentioned my boyfriend to her, she seemed blank as ever.

I knew I should keep away for a few days to give my boyfriend's family time to recover, but I needed the evenings too much to do it. I needed those seats on the decking, the talk of the moon.

They asked about my mother sometimes, not out of politeness but genuine concern. I didn't have much to tell them. She was a mystery to me as she was to herself.

My boyfriend never asked about her. I think that when he found people, their actions, their behaviour, distressing, he pretended that he had not noticed—he never asked about my mother, and he never mentioned Berezi's husband, not once since the time he hit the dog at the lake.

Sometimes I thought I missed my boyfriend's mother. I didn't know why. I had never met her. My boyfriend did not talk about her. Berezi showed me photographs one day when the house was quiet. She and their older brother were born before; my boyfriend and Lur were born once they'd moved here. I saw how their mother was beautiful. I saw her in my boyfriend's face. I thought I heard her when Berezi was talking. She was missing Euskara. She was reading their folklore. She talked about it on the decking and Aitor shook his head. The Basque people are called Euskaldunak, Berezi said, which means speakers of Euskara. They have lived in their land, Euskal Herria, since forever. The world is a god named Amalur. Every morning, she births the sun. Every night, the sun returns to her womb, travels through the red seas beneath the earth. Every night, Amalur births the moon. This is a cycle without ending. This is the world.

I thought I heard their mother then.

My boyfriend did not like to listen. I think he thought a lot of his brother, the one in America. This is a guess. He would never have said. I think that maybe he did not like to think about how things had been, before. I think that maybe he did not remember the language as well as he might have; it had been many years since they had spoken it together. Sometimes he was there when Aitor told stories—the language was banned, it was illegal to give your child a Basque name, illegal to teach the language or learn it, and they fined us, Aitor said, they fined us for speaking it, our own language, in our own land, the government removed the language even from graves—sometimes my boyfriend was there but, when I looked at him, I saw the expression he had. I saw the light on his face from the phone in his palm. I knew he did not want to know.

Berezi had another baby, a year after the first. This baby was called Xixili. When this baby needed injections, Berezi left Ihintza with us. Ihintza knew us very well. She never made strange. We had only to keep her until Berezi returned.

But Berezi didn't come. Her husband showed up instead. He came through into the kitchen and the baby was then fractious, running around on the kitchen tiles. My boyfriend cleared his throat. Ihintza was running, as best she could.

That's enough, Berezi's husband yelled at her, stop it! Shut up!

He yelled with his chest.

Then Berezi's husband screamed at the baby, screamed terrible, adult things.

The baby stopped moving. She stood very still.

I hated this man.

My boyfriend started a conversation with him. I think he hoped, that if so engaged, the man couldn't yell at the baby again, but I hated it, anyway. I hated it all. My boyfriend and I stood there and I hated us both because we had known who he was, we had known what would happen, we had known since the first time we saw him hit his own dog. But even then, my boyfriend had said, I hate when he does that. This time he didn't say anything. Berezi's husband left and we were the two of us in the kitchen and I realised, I knew, that he would never acknowledge it. I think it was too big.

During this period I am thinking of, I was always at my boyfriend's house. I felt I had known him forever there. This night, it was dinner—Berezi was excited about a group she had joined that had calls on Zoom three times a week to speak together in Basque—it is a language isolate, unrelated to any other—my boyfriend was clearing plates away, their stepmother was heading straight out onto the decking. We were older, then, but only just. Berezi had the babies now; Lur was fifteen and had Berezi's dog turning circles, standing to beg; their stepmother was five cigarettes deep into a reclaimed habit and we were trying to put her off: think of the phlegm, think of the cough. It wasn't warm out the back. It rarely was. Even warm days became cold because then there was no cloud to hold the heat in. We sat outside on the seats, there were various blankets, and it was quiet so my boyfriend got a speaker and played music through his phone. His father said, that's my boy, at the music he chose and my boyfriend was elated. He looked down at his hands.

In the pause between songs, Aitor said he heard owls.

I didn't notice his little sister, but she had sat down beside me, and while my boyfriend was inside, on the hunt for a speaker, she said, Can I add you on Snapchat?

Her name was Lur. She was younger and she didn't speak much when I was there. She had purple glasses and purple braces on little teeth, like a child I'd babysit. I was told she had been very close to their mother. Apparently they looked very alike, Lur being the double of their mother as a child; it was in her face and her little teeth. I heard that relations had, at times, slipped up and called the child Maritxu, instead of Lur.

Lur said to me on this night, can I add you on Snapchat?

In fact, she said, Please?

I didn't say anything. Because we were side by side but both looking ahead, I felt we were like spies in those British movies, sat back-to-back together in a park. Aitor, when he heard them, exclaimed about the owls. He had explained to me that Lur was small because Maritxu had died. They were connected. It was something he truly believed. Berezi had Ihintza. She was pointing at the moon, just born.

Okay, I said.

Lur went inside early. She said she was tired. When I was leaving the house, I walked away from their Wi-Fi connection but even then I had, waiting from her, three Snapchat notifications. I didn't open them until I was in my own house, in the kitchen with a kettle boiling.

They were like this:

> *Hi this is lur*
>
> *Maybe this is weird but i need to talk to u*
>
> *I am pregnant can i talk to u about it*

I'm not sure why but I felt like I could cry and cry. Maybe you have to have met her then. Lur was so small—glasses and braces—her mother was dead and she missed her so much—she was quiet even with her sister, her brother—Berezi had babies but her husband screamed at them—here she was, now, sending me messages on this app so that there could be no trail, the messages would disappear—it crushed me up, I stood in the kitchen, still.

> *I said: ofc u can Lur, u can talk to me ab anything*
>
> *Does ur family know?*

Three or four hours later, my mother came into the kitchen. She jumped when she saw me. In fact, she screamed and almost fell back. Then she said, teary, What the fuck are you doing here? and I said, I live here, though in fact I knew what she meant. Why are you in the kitchen at this time of night? Why aren't you sleeping, like you usually are?

I said I couldn't sleep, though truthfully I hadn't tried.

My mother was at the kettle, filling it.

I don't know how long Lur had carried her secret for, but I knew, seeing my mother, that I would tell her in minutes. I'm not sure why. She and I, we weren't close. We didn't have conversations, we didn't eat together, we didn't say good night to each other before we slept. We shared a feeling of having survived terrible people but relief couldn't bond us together and we lived our lives some significant distance apart. I said, Can I tell you something?

Sometimes my mother acted as though she couldn't hear. She did not turn around.

Can I tell you something, a secret?

She poured her hot water. She said, If you want.

My boyfriend's little sister, she says that she's pregnant.

My mother said she was tired. She said that I should go to bed.

The next night I was at their house, Lur wasn't around. Berezi was there with her babies who ate food with their hands. Aitor loved them, sometimes he asked them questions in Basque. That night on the deck, the owls were loud and their stepmother brought out an unopened dessert wine she'd found. She said it would be horrible but it was wine after all. We all took tiny, tiny cups. It was something between vinegar and honey. Aitor told us things about the owls. I was almost sleeping, to tell the truth, my back flat against the chair. Berezi passed me the baby she had named Xixili, her little body leaden with sleep, and she said, You girls can nap together. I was almost sleeping, my mouth wide open, my boyfriend always making a face at me when I snapped back awake. I was listening. I thought of gods: the earth, the sun, the moon. Xixili lay on my lap, breathing in and breathing out. Native languages have a value, their stepmother said. Yes, Aitor said. I believe this, Berezi said, this is Musa Anter: if my mother tongue is shaking the foundations of your state, it probably means that you built your state on my land.

Before I left, I said, Where's Lur?

My boyfriend shrugged. He said, She's almost sixteen.

Aitor said, I think she is upstairs, sleeping. She's tired these days. The teenage years are hard.

When I got home, my mother wasn't in the house.

I had four messages on Snapchat, they were like this:

> *No one knows*
>
> *Dont tell them*
>
> *Im sorry if this is weird*
>
> *I just thought i shld say to someone and ur always around*

My alarm went off but I just lay there sleeping. I wanted light dreams, the ones that come through like films on your eyelids, when the room is bright but you're still sleeping; in this vague, bright way, I dreamt that somebody loved me. The feeling coloured the rest of my day.

My mother was out.

I sat in the kitchen.

I struggled to reply to Lur's messages. I didn't know how to be a friend to her. I asked her things like a nurse might. I didn't know who she was, how to speak to her. The pauses between her replies consumed my day.

Lur wanted to meet. She wanted to go to a café. She asked me to go up to the counter for both of us because she said ordering made her trip up on her words. She seemed alright. She had her hair (dark and curly) kept back in places with purple clips. She took off her glasses for a bit because the coffee was so hot it steamed them up.

How are you doing? I said, my voice soft like a nurse.

I'm confused, Lur said. I'm sleepy. But I'm not afraid.

She's only little, I thought. She hadn't even finished school.

Lur asked, do you think I should tell them?

I thought of my boyfriend. I said, I don't know.

I wanted to know if she remembered what Berezi had said, that the world is just a parent. I imagined their mother, imagined her taking Lur's tiny hand, saying, Listen, the sun is the earth's baby, reborn every day. When I looked at Lur I thought repeatedly that she was little, far too little. I knew that they believed Lur had been stunted by grief.

We lived in a small place. My boyfriend rang me. He said, Why were you getting coffee with my little sister? She's fifteen.

I lied. I said, Me and your sister, I think we're friends.

Sometimes at their house—where things were light and easy—sometimes things were so good I felt like I was floating on it—things were so good, it was like, paradisiacal—it was small things, it was out on the deck when everyone was laughing, full of sugar—when the moon was really bright and the flowers were out—when my boyfriend took out his speaker and he put on music and I felt it in my chest, in my heart, how much I loved living, I loved being alive—sometimes at their house, I felt this: pure elation.

So maybe I knew for a while that I loved my boyfriend's family and not him. I liked my boyfriend very much: he was beautiful, calm, he never raised his voice, but he was just one of the pieces of that family I adored. It was his whole family I loved.

We didn't work without his family, that was the truth.

My mother was out and I called him to come over. I said I'd make dinner. We sat in my kitchen and I fucked up making pasta and he went to set the table but there was nothing to set it with, only a few forks, small plates—he played music from his phone and the sound was bad—when we were eating, he looked around, he seemed like a photocopy of himself: pale, fuzzy.

I talked because the noise of just the music was making me cagey, I said, Doesn't it stress you out when you see Ihintza, Xixili, getting so big so fast? They just get so big, it's so scary, they keep growing and growing—I just, you know, I read ages one to three are crucial, they hardwire a person for life, everything is formed in those first thirty-six months—it sets you up and I think, it's so sad—the schools here, you know, it's just tarmac and they're inside all the time—sit down and shut up, and wear what we tell you, have your hair how we tell you, even when they get home, they have other stupid stuff to do—I guess I do hate schools, at least, I hate them here—did you read that link I sent, the Forever Chemicals, they're going to kill us all, it said, they said there could be complete infertility by twenty-forty-five, I'm serious—the plastic's in the water, in the food, it's in your blood!

My boyfriend said he wasn't hungry. The food was that bad.

Lur messaged and we met in the café again. I ordered our drinks. She sat with one of her knees bent up under her. It's okay, she said, I'm kind of excited. That's why I told you. It's going round and round in my head. I thought I should tell someone and then I can say this stuff out loud.

She wanted a girl, so that she could name the baby Maritxu. That was important. She was supposed to be worried and I reassuring, but I found her to be happy—ready she said—

and I felt fear was dripping from my mouth like spit. I couldn't stop talking. I told her what I had seen, what I'd read. People die having babies, I said. Even here, even now, people die giving birth. In my head, all my thoughts, I was thinking and thinking. Whoever you are, someone birthed you. You grew in the dark waters of a belly, of a body, you walked around with someone for the guts of a year, your shape was covered by their skin, their organs, their clothes. I thought of what Berezi said, their old religion, the sun and moon, babies, born every morning and night.

I said, Lur, are you sleeping?

She said, Babe, are you?

I wasn't, really.

I only had light, airy dreams. They didn't fill me up.

She said she hoped the baby was a girl, that she could call her Maritxu. It might seem strange on a newborn, she said, but she'd grow into it, like their mother had.

I was all in my head. Whoever you are, this is where you began.

I saw my mother, briefly. She had lost her job. It was weeks later and there were no new messages from Lur (they stopped as they'd started: one night there, one night not). My mother said, I was thinking about what you said, about your boyfriend's sister. When I was giving birth, they always said to me, you waited too long, it's too difficult, you should have done this much, much younger.

I said, are they allowed to say stuff like that?

My mother was tired. She said, I didn't report them.

She wasn't well. I couldn't leave her. I knew that it was all burning up.

The next time I saw my boyfriend, we sat in a café, then

walked round a park. When he looked at me, I felt he was wondering how he had come to know me. I thought he was breaking up with me when he said he had news, but in fact the news was that his little sister was pregnant.

Lur? I said, surprised that he knew.

Then he did break up with me. It was a few hours later. I could tell he was thinking about it, trying to see if I was okay before he did. He was assessing me. We didn't argue.

I knew that he knew I loved his whole family.

I knew, even then, that I would miss them for the rest of my life.

I found it difficult. I struggled, a little, to live. Imagine: no more dinners, no more nights. I was in the flat with my mother, who stayed in her bed. There were no voices, there was no food, no music. I tried to dream of the chairs on the decking but it was not in my power. All I had was the flat with my mother in it. I sat in the kitchen and nobody ever came in. I sat on my own and I thought it all through. I wanted to know: did they think of me? I thought about Lur. Sometimes I stared at the space where our conversation had lived, all of our words and their invisible tracks. I wanted to message her but I couldn't do it.

I saw Berezi maybe five months later. She had Xixili with her, the child's dark curly hair up in bunches. We talked for a long time. I thought that maybe she missed me from the way that she spoke, from the way that she told me to rest up, to keep going. We talked for a long time until she mentioned her husband. I had to leave her then, his name causing me pain. I said that I was in a rush, and I went home to my mother. She was in her room. She had her eyes closed tight. I was annoyed at myself, and her, and I talked straight at her but I knew from her breathing that I was making her worse so I left. I sat in the kitchen until morning.

Yes, it was grieving. I grieved who I might have been.

I missed my mother.

Since I was a teenager, she'd broken in my shoes for me. She insisted. I had seen her feet bleed. She wore the shoes just until they softened, and would never hurt me.

Mary

I

You are here because Christy is gentle. You told him that you lost your job and he said, immediately, that they're all fuckers anyway and they don't deserve you and they'll be lost without you which made you feel, for an evening, that it could be true. He tells you it's fine, that this is the beauty of his work—because he does lifts and taxis and takeaway deliveries at night (cash)—he can work all the hours he wants, all the hours that youse need. You are here because later, maybe four days later, he says that you're not out and about much, are you? And then two days after that, he starts talking about this uncle that did a creative writing class at the Presbyterian Church Hall. It looks like it's running again, he says. 'And it'd be good to get out of the house, wouldn't it, dote?' This is what he says.

You go to the classes. You go every Tuesday three weeks in a row, take one bus there and one bus back. You sit on the church hall's fold-out seat and you say nothing and you struggle because the other people, they did this same course before the summer together; on the first Tuesday, the instructor knew everyone but you by name. You struggle because, in the breaks, they talk about people you could not know and they look at you, if they look at you, as though you are no different from any other stranger, as though you have not heard their stories, as though you do not remember what they wrote, what it means. You look at them, you think: how can youse be so unfriendly? You have told me everything. We are already friends.

You think about the job you lost almost without end. You feel in waves both the weighted crushing panic of it and something sharper, something more embarrassing, something like hurt, or loneliness, or grief. Those people you worked with, they bought you a birthday cake. They each had signed their name on a card.

You take the bus and, almost every week, there is the same child. You notice today (Tuesday; Week 4). You see it suddenly, violently—there is the same child here, every time. Everyone knows her name. You see it like this: there is a child at the front and they are calling out to her. At their stop, she walks one couple right up the bus. 'Bye, Mary,' they say to her, heading out the doors. She has been here every week, you realise. 'Night, petal,' they say.

You want to write about her in your class. The feeling almost fills you up. You go to the Presbyterian Church Hall and you sit on your fold-out seat and when your instructor (guide, is the word they use) says, 'Who wants to tell us about their project?', you say, 'I do.' You feel good about it. You feel that the others swivel their heads towards you, that they are impressed by the way you speak these words. You say, 'I do. I have this idea about a child, maybe on a train or a bus. Maybe she's there all the time.'

'What do you mean by that?' says the instructor.

Mary

You feel panic, then. The floor, the seat, begin to seep away. Your face is painful. Why do youse hate me? you think. You want to say: youse'd just have to see her. I can't put words on it yet. But you cannot admit that the child is real. It is a creative writing class. You have to have made her up. You cannot say that you've just seen her. You cannot say: These middle-aged women got on and you guess they're used to having children with them because they said, Two adult tickets, please, and the child was standing there, right at the front, and she said, 'No shit!' when they said that, and the people on the bus, all round you, laughed; and you felt as though you were trespassing, gate-crashing, as though you were somewhere you had no right to be, that you felt this ache, almost homesick, listening to the laughter; you cannot say: she was just on my bus, I just saw her. She got off at the stop nearest the high school and ran to the chippie called Taste of Peking and got herself a paper bag of something that steamed with heat when she opened it back in her seat, and the paper was lit translucent with grease, and the bus waited for her, we all waited, we all watched her running.

You say, you say: 'It's just an image, right now.'

You do the exercises you are asked to do, you use the writing prompt which is a two-pence coin. In the break, you hear someone saying that their grandmother, god rest their soul, believed with their whole being that Earth is Hell, that this is the suffering, that this is the damnation. 'So I'm thinking of doing something with that,' they say.

You miss Christy very badly. He is destroyed with the tiredness, the both of youse know it. He likes to leave you voicemails. You like to listen to them. He leaves you one this week that says: and it's like, fuck, this is just one chapter, dote, right, and you'd never stop a film halfway through and say fuck this film is shocking, you'd keep watching, and you know, well, some people do stop a film, right, but—

You are here for him. You are here so that he says, 'Every cloud has a silver lining,' about the lost job and he can say nice things about your becoming a writer, about how happy he is that you've been out of the house. Week 2, the instructor asked, before the class started, where you work and if you're married, and you answered only the second question because even to talk about Christy brings you that flush of relief, of peace, of comfort, and you tell the instructor that you met him when you were young, when you were fourteen, when you were dressed in your friend's clothes to go out and you went out and there in a garden, in somebody's garden, were boys huddled together and there was one turned away from youse who looked, hands running up and down his back, as though he was being kissed, and youse were staring, then, as he turned round, hands falling down, and it was just him, and youse realised it was a joke, his own hands rubbing his own back. 'Christy—' said your friend, someone who knew him then. He smiled with his teeth and they glowed in the astronomical dusk. 'Well, then. What's happening?' he said.

II

Week 7, the instructor says slowly, 'I don't think it's working. What you have to decide is: is she a character, this child? And then you have to flesh her out. Or is she a symbol? Is she a metaphor? You have to decide what you're doing. It's—you don't seem sure in yourself.'

You see Christy Wednesday night. You see him, you love

even, you think, the whites of his eyes, you would know any cell of him, to you they would all have his name. He had a great fare today, he tells you, an insane fare; he got, he tells you: three-hundred-and-eighty-four-pounds.

This is crazy.

You say it, you say, 'What? How?' and he beams at you.

He says, 'Some day for one day!'

He has bought you things on the way home: chocolate you have not bought in over two months; wine; meat, good meat. He puts the things on the table, all the time smiling. You say, 'I don't understand.' He says, 'It's a good thing, dote. It's all good.' You feel happiness that sits very tight in your chest. He sings silly, making his voice waver: Things Can Only Get Better! He puts his arms, the skin warm and the hairs standing on end, round you. He sings that one line four times in total. He sways you with him. Things! Can Only Get! BETTER! The last time, he punches the air.

He calls the takeaway places he drives for to say that he's sick, that he can't do tonight. He smiles at you as he says it, as he coughs. Tonight, he cooks. You can hardly stand the smell, it's so good. You open the wine. You open the chocolate. You repeat to yourself, I don't understand it, but you mean it in a sense of bliss, a sense of wonder. You find yourself listing adjectives to describe these foods; this is the writing class, you feel, its anchor starting to sink into the silt of your brain. Light, you think. Melodic. The wine, you would say, it dances. He takes some of the chocolate, goes back to the pan. He groans. He says, 'God, that's good.' Eating this chocolate, you would tell the instructor, you feel saved. Maybe it's bad, you think, bad writing. But you aren't embarrassed.

At the table, he talks about other days. You look at his face, at the outline of him. You eat the food. You drink the wine. You have not drunk in over two months and so the wine has an impact. You think three-word sentences over and over, things like: Here We Are, things like: This Is It. He talks about other days and you realise, suddenly, that it has been a long time since you have heard him speak like this. There is never time. And you feel grief for the nights that youse could have been having, but have not had, since you lost the job.

I miss you.

You say it to him. It seems to sting. He says, 'It's a good day, dote. Let it be good.'

You will, you say. You will let it be good.

Youse have finished eating but are still sat, drinking. 'So the fare today,' he says. 'I got a call first thing, I mean first thing this morning: would you drive this man to the other end of the country?' He sits up straight.

Perhaps, says the wine, he feels something like a hunter-gatherer. He has travelled, he has returned, youse have consumed everything together. You are drunk, you realise.

'So the first shock, I go to the pick-up address and there's no man, there's these three girls. They're young, they've got suitcases, they're literally wanting to go from here to there, like, edge to edge.' He uses his fingers in the air to demonstrate the distance. Picture the country, he implies, with his worn hands spread. They are going a distance as far as it is possible to go. 'I've been told to be strict as about payment and everything because of the distance involved, you know? How are they paying, that's the thing. Well, you want to see the amount of cash these kids have. I ring the guy at dispatch because they said to pick up a man and I says, look, there's these girls here, teenagers really, early-early twenties at the most, and I says, is this right? And he says, sure, look, if they're the people wanting to go, it's probably their da booked it for them or whoever, right, so that's grand, and they get in and we head off.'

It's a long story. It's a long day. The drive lasts about five hours. They stop at two petrol stations for them to pee. The girls, the women, they talk among themselves but not in a language that Christy has. He puts on music and they dance in the back using some of the moves he says we'd've done in a primary school disco, big-fish-little-fish-cardboard-boxing and feeding ducks, and they buy him a coffee at one of the stops with some of the cash they have. About three hours in, the strangest thing happens, Christy says. They get a phone call, one of the girls does, and she holds the phone out so that the others can hear.

'Where the fuck are you?' shouts a man.

The girls tense. They ask Christy. Christy names the town closest to them.

'You're fucking late,' the man shouts, an older man, and he's livid. 'You're late already, you're going to be even fucking later. You all better be here in the next three hours or there's going to be trouble, do you understand me? There is going to be serious, serious fucking trouble.'

The mood in the car is bad after that.

Christy says that he said, 'So who was that then?' and the girls look at each other and then one of them says: 'Friend.' He says that he said, 'Why are youse heading down this way again?' and the same girl says, firmly: 'Beauty Contest.' And he says, 'A beauty contest that starts at this time of the day on a Wednesday in a port-town?' The girl says: 'Beauty Contest.' And she says, 'Fast, please.'

She repeats that at intervals, sounding something like scared. 'Car, Christy. Fast, please.'

You look at Christy. He is not looking at you. He looks at the table, at the wall. He says, 'I would have, I mean, I would have taken them to a police station or the airport, anywhere they asked. But they didn't ask.'

He is confessing, you realise.

'I would have helped them,' he says again. But how can he say that? Because he did not help them. He drove the car until it stopped.

Later, he says this, he whispers: 'Are you angry with me?'

The question makes you feel it. You are detached because of the drinking. You are somewhere deeper inside your body. You feel the touch of him on your skin. You say, 'I love you,' because you feel that you need to say it while you still can, while it's still true. You feel the heat of loathing inside yourself, a burn of disgust. How are you here, you think, how is this happening? How can it be that he isn't good?

You do not sleep. You get up and you sit in the bathroom with the lights off because they make too much noise on. But this is, says the wine, how men are. The bad ones are bad and the good ones are passive. He would not have hurt those girls—you know this, this is true—yet he helped others to hurt them. He would not hurt you but maybe he would not stop another. He does not say he is sorry because he does not really believe he has done anything.

So he cannot be brave, you say, should I hate him for that?

You take the bus that goes past the Presbyterian Church Hall that Thursday though the class isn't on. It is Thursday, not Tuesday. You sit on a seat near the back and then you decide to sit upstairs and watch the streets and the houses from a height. Mary is stood on the stairs, swinging off the handrail. The bus moves at speed but she swings into each corner; she hangs in the air, her arms taut. She is no more than nine. You remember nine: remember the belief that your mother, when you saw her, could do real true magic; remember the girl who moved to your class from a school in London and told youse that she had sex with her ten-year-old boyfriend, remember confusion and the denial of confusion, and the small hard worry that nested in your body, and how each of youse told others, as youse understood the London-girl intended youse to do. You feel, suddenly, huge sadness for who you were as a child. Your mother, you thought that she could remove portions of her fingers at will.

You say, 'Mary, can I sit upstairs?'

The child says: 'Full.'

She looks at you. She knows that everybody knows her name. She has this confidence that each week you struggle to describe. She knows people, she knows everyone, she knows that she is known. She is protected: when anyone linked with the bus company, an inspector, someone linked with the council, gets on, she calmly, quietly, sits beside an adult, any adult, and appears to be with them, and they do that for her. You include yourself in that. Hanging there, she reminds you of photographs you have seen of islanders, barefoot, climbing down cliffs to collect birds' eggs.

'Sit!' yells somebody from below. 'Mary! Get yourself sat, right now!'

You have never been on this part of the route before; you passed the church hall several stops back. Youse are approaching the motorway, where the bus will drive on the hard shoulder at an entirely new speed. 'Mary!' yells the bus driver. She skips up the steps to where there are seats.

You climb to the top deck after her. You sit right at the back. Everything runs past you. You applied for three jobs today before you left the house. Each one took hours. You do not think of Christy. You think of some place, the thought of which has always been calming, a place that is warm and dark and still. You are there now, you imagine. At the last class, you read out what you had written. Mary is like, you wrote, some headmaster's son: they know they belong. At the last class, a woman said: 'How can you associate this child with freedom, anyway? I don't get it. You say it yourself, she's stuck on a bus.'

III

You take the classes seriously. You spend hours every day choking on words. They don't respect you because you will not pick a new project. 'It was great to get you started, to get you talking,' says the instructor. 'But it doesn't have to be this one, does it?' The tone is pleading. 'We all have false starts, we all have things we abandon and come back to, maybe years later. It's an image you had, a strong image even, but you have other stories inside you. We just need to tease them out.' But it is this one. You have to tell them about it.

The hall smells cold. When people speak their voices echo a little and you feel certain that they are not using their true accents, that they are using different words and intonations. The instructor explains a new device they would like youse to try: Flashback. 'It gives context, it gives background, it makes us grow with the characters,' they say. At the break, you take two biscuits from the plate, and then three, and then four, and then you go to the toilet which is down a corridor to the right of the stage to change your tampon and you sit on the toilet, your body deadened with cramps, until you hear someone else come down the hall and how their footsteps stop at the toilet door and then you hurry, you have to hurry to let them in.

You are asked to work for some minutes with this new device, the flashback, but instead you write, feeling something like fury, about the bus, its damp air, the steep stairs climbing up. You feel focused, terribly focused, seeing things: the sweat on the handrail, the clump of hair rolling round gently on the floor, the grease marking the window where someone's head rested as they slept; you sit on the fold-out chair, feel its metal legs and fabric covering. You write even as the instructor announces the exercise over, as they say, expectantly, that it is time to move on. Your face doesn't feel like your face with this tension, you can feel your skin scrumpled, feel your teeth ache, and you write still about the sound of laughter when it happens, you write still about the prams Mary helps mothers to negotiate through the doors, about the bus's rattling movement which rocks you. And you realise, slowly, that you have caused a disruption. The class is speaking and they are speaking of you. There are questions, and the instructor is frustrated, angry that you have ruined the rhythm, and they let the questions fall, they are not mediating. 'You don't even describe her, there's nothing about what she looks like, you can't picture her at all,' they say, as though anything is important about what someone looks like rather than what, than who, they are; you feel sicker, maybe, than you have ever felt, and there is a man, a man who sits forward on the edge of his fold-out seat and says: 'But if she's real, if she's a character not a symbol, wouldn't you need to report it to someone? That could be the plot, you could use that, what happens; the narrator contacts the authorities. I mean, there isn't a plot at the minute, it's just—you're just on the bus. But that could be the story, that could be what happens.' You hate him. You look at the instructor, the one who could make them stop.

'Maybe,' says the instructor, 'the bus inspector finds out?'

They are commended.

'Now, there's an idea!' says the first man. 'Maybe the inspector comes on one day and nobody lets the wee girl sit beside them and he asks—' You told them that she moves to hide, to sit with youse.

You say: 'Worry about your own fucking story! Worry about your own fucking life! What are you doing here, anyway? Everything you write is about a middle-aged man and these women throwing themselves at him, it's just paragraphs and paragraphs about tight dresses and you hating your wife. It's fucking weird and don't you dare talk about Mary, don't, you don't—'

There you are: screaming.

He doesn't look wounded enough so you say: 'You make me sick.'

And it's true that you are sick: here you are, almost retching.

You stand and you realise, violently, how much you have bled. You have bled through everything, the thick denim of your trousers, deep into the fabric of the fold-away seat. You stand in the hall and the members of the class look at you, saying not a word, and then you leave and you know that they watch you going, stare at the seat you've left in your wake, and you feel, though perhaps it makes no sense, something sharp like betrayal that not one of those people stood up, tried to help. Outside, it is darkening. Here she is, the winter. Taking no buses, no taxi, the walk home takes an hour and nine minutes. It is cold and your lungs are destroyed with a stitch. Why do youse hate me? you think. You do not understand it.

At home, it is like you have never seen: clumps and clots and all this blood.

There is so much that you think, something is happening. But there are words you will never say, even in a half-whisper. What good is it to know what things are, what lies beneath the appearance of them? It is nothing until it is stated. It is nothing if it is not named. It is just blood, like you have never seen before.

You receive a warning from the instructor. It's there, the next morning. This is a final warning. You must be able to take criticism. You must be able to listen. You must not get personal. I must inform you that you are only being given this chance considering your apparent ill-health in the last class.

You took Mary's bus on the way in. You were tired already then, but you thought it'd be fleeting. You listened to a voicemail from Christy: We'll be okay dote, yeah? Everything is going to be fine, you wait, we—

The bus was quieter than usual. There were just four other heads sitting round you. She came up the back. 'Question,' she said. She reached for the necklace you wear round your neck, the locket. She wanted to see inside. You opened it for her, you showed her the faces. It is packed with many tiny images, people laughing, laughing, laughing. 'Who?' she said, pointing at the people.

You don't know who they are. You bought the locket like that.

IV

You let yourself cry once. O my fucking god, you scream. You see the girls in the back of Christy's car, watch him driving. He turns round in his seat, he says: 'Where is it youse're going?' He takes them to the man, he drives them the whole fucking way. He comes home to you.

'I would have helped them,' he says. He does not say he's sorry. He does not say he's done wrong. And he looks at you, the way he looks at you, you know what he's saying: he did it for you. Who else needs the money? Who else lost their job?

He makes you complicit.

You are just like everyone else, you think. He moves to hold you. You still allow it. Isn't the truth that we all do terrible things? We are just like everyone else. You look at it once and then never again. Then you say, my boyfriend, once he drove these girls five hours for a beauty contest! Three-hundred-and-eighty-pound fare. Isn't it mad what people will do?

Some things have to be looked at, not studied. 'I mean, the name,' says a woman. 'Is the story set in a time when that name was everywhere? Like what, the seventies, the eighties? Is it that this is a super common name and she's, like, representing children in general? Or is it set when that name's become unusual for children, when that would be notable?' The instructor says that this is a great point, that names contain multitudes, hidden meanings, hidden depths. There is a pause. Then the instructor says to you, 'Are you—are you still thinking?'

So it's me, you think. Still me who has to understand. And why would you even know the answer? What year is it, what time is it, what era is this—the best it has ever been? Are we safe? Who would ask you? How could you know?

Not everything can be felt. Some things are just to be looked at. This is a deliberate practice, one that you cultivate. It is the act of not-seeing. It is the work of pretence. To see the truth of things, people pick at them. This is what you refuse. You want only to see the surface of things. The world has to be let wash over you.

Of course you can see where they are coming from: the child does no homework, she does not play with friends; of course you can see that, if you study it, there will have to come from her, at some point, an adult, that there will be consequences, that the adult will have issues, that there will be hurt or loneliness or grief, but this is not something which you can bear.

'Why can't you just look at what I'm showing you?' you shouted in the class that night. 'It isn't always sad! It doesn't always have meaning! There's this child and youse don't know how but she's always on the bus. It was her birthday last Thursday and it's Tuesday today and she's still wearing the huge silver badge that came with a card: *Hip Hip Hooray! Nine Today!*'

Every time the bus stops, she moves back a seat to tell the joke she's learnt to someone else and everyone is laughing or smiling or trying when she says it, even though everyone can hear her every time. She moves back another seat, she tells the same joke for the ninth time. 'That's hilarious!' we say. 'Haha! Good one, Mary!' We are smiling, we are laughing, we all hear her say it.

Tell it again, Mary. Tell it again.

Russia

I DON'T KNOW WHERE I AM

He is on his way to the psychic who works on Bloomfield Avenue. He's booked an appointment with them on the recommendation of a neighbour, the one who child-minds in her adjacent one-bed flat.

The neighbour sees him one day on the stairs and the way she looks at him, he has to say, How's it going, and she says, Well, you know the way I've never taken a shower my whole life, the thing makes me shake and cry and throw up, and it's difficult, you understand, life-limiting, in fact, to always need access to a bath, to bathe, well, this psychic's after telling me that it's not my fault at all, it's my mother, my mother used to put us in a cold shower as a punishment when we done wrong, not that we even really done any wrong, you understand, she was a headcase and she was horrible and I'm glad that she's dead.

He says, The psychic knew? And the neighbour says: Once it was said, then that second, I mean, that very second, I remembered, I knew it was right. She did, she used to put us in the cold shower and we'd be screaming, and it winter, and she fucking did it, the fucker.

Who's the psychic? he says. And she looks at him, wondering if he is taking the piss. They've never spoken before, except to say: How's things, and: Grand, grand. He sees her on the stairs, scrapping with various children. They're on Bloomfield Avenue, she says. That's them there.

It's a small set-up above a hardware store with brooms and plastic flower baskets set out on the pavement. He presses the buzzer, climbs the narrow carpeted stairs, sits on one of the three office chairs set out as a waiting-room, takes a cupful of plastic water from the dispenser. There's an old smell of incense, and the click of an intermittent automated air freshener, and the pale sound of harp music playing through a Bluetooth speaker and cars passing, spitting old rain up from puddles. There're posters on the walls about healing circles and meditation and sacred sessions, the discreet promise of ayahuasca, of drugs. He's worried about seeing someone he knows, about being embarrassed, but he finds the emptiness distressing, too; here he is, he thinks, the only fucker stupid enough to be here.

The psychic says, What brings you to me?

He says, Aren't you supposed to know?

The psychic says: Everyone, no word of a lie, every single person says that. You've, none of youse, you've no concept of how this works.

They look at each other.

What's your name? he says.

Ursa, the psychic says.

Is that your real name? he says.

I don't think that's polite, says the psychic. He hears the click of the air-freshener. There's also no good answer. A real name, you mean, did I choose it or did someone choose it for me? Why should you care either way? What difference could it make to you?

I don't know how this works, he says.

No, says the psychic. Fuck me, I can see that much.

How does it work? he says, eventually.

It depends. It depends on the person. It depends how open they are, how clear they are on what they want. You, I don't think you're clear at all. You don't—I mean, there's people come in and they've one clear question. Do I marry him? Is she going to live? Even bigger questions, you know, what should I do? It's big and it's vague but it's one thing, it's one query. You, I mean, you don't have one question, you have thousands. You're—the way you are, everything's a question.

Yeah, he says.

That wasn't a question, said the psychic. I wasn't asking you. I can see it. Listen, you can't play Where's Wally if you don't know what Wally looks like. The psychic sighs. But we can try have a look around, see what we see. We might find eventually you go, O my days, there he is. I knew him once. That guy's Wally.

You don't need to dumb it down, he says.

The psychic flicks their eyes to the ceiling. Listen, says the psychic, we're only after meeting. Let's not expect too much. I want you to tell me one thing. I want you to think of—it's not nice, this, but we all feel guilty about something, okay, and we all have some image that makes us wince, that stings, you know, I mean I know there's an image in your head as I'm saying this now. And I want you to share that with me.

He is surprised by the panic he feels, the sharpness in his

throat. I don't want to, he wants to say, but he can't. He says, I thought you were going to tell me things, I didn't know I'd have to tell you.

Yeah, says the psychic. I said it, youse all do it, youse come in with no concept of how this works. Look, you were thinking of something there. Just say it. You'll feel better if you do.

And it's true that the word GUILT did bring to him an image. He has a sister, he is thinking.

He looks behind the psychic, at the painted wall.

He has a sister and he hates watching her brush her hair. However she does it, she creates more tats with every stroke. She keeps her hair long, very long, long enough that people make assumptions about her, about its purpose or meaning, and the way she brushes it, she makes it knot and tangle in other places, creates these huge tats of mess, and it's frustrating, infuriating to watch her, to watch it get worse, and he feels, sometimes, that she's done this all through her life, all of it, making it painful, making it difficult, making it hurt.

You never offered to brush it for her, says the psychic.

It startles him. She would never have let me, he says. I was her brother, it would be weird, it would be, I couldn't've done that.

Still, says the psychic, you wish you'd helped.

There's an electric heater in the corner, and a bucket to catch water dripping through the ceiling tiles. I don't know what you're talking about, he says.

This is going to take a while, says the psychic. And, let's be honest, pal, you need this. I'm only going to charge you for every second session. There's a calendar out in the hall, just write your first name down for whenever suits you next. I'm away to Edinburgh for a long weekend in two weeks' time, but you'll know yourself, just don't be putting your name on the days with an X through.

Right, he says. He stands to go. Cheers, he says to the psychic. Thanks.

BURY YOUR DEAD

He does not find the first flowers. He finds what he supposes are the first flowers: there is the skull of a Viking, the gaping fracture which proved fatal still painfully visible, on the third floor, and he finds, on the floor in a circle around the display-case, clumps of gorse, wildflowers of the kind that grow on verges: cow-parsley, rosebay willowherb, ragwort. There is a small piece of paper, folded over into a card, a candle drawn on its front. Inside says, BURY YOUR DEAD. He tells no one but Sinéad, who he sees as he's gathering the pulled stems together, and who says, This has happened before, you know. He doesn't know, but she tells him.

The first flowers are found by Sinéad, who gets Brian from Security. The first flowers are white and they spell, in capital letters, M-U-M, and they are found by the Egyptian exhibit, on top of the clear box in which the preserved body of a twenty-six-year-old woman is kept. Sinéad takes a sweet tea in the staff-room but she's angry rather than shocked. Repeatedly she says, What the fuck's that supposed to mean? Their manager, Yusuf, comes down and asks Sinéad for a detailed description of what happened that morning. I turned the corner, Sinéad says, her voice tight with frustration. I saw flowers of the kind that are used in funerals, placed in a hearse, left on a grave, flowers that spell out, in three letters, M-U-M.

Yusuf says, we are the only ones that know, correct? Myself, yourself, and Brian? We will keep it among ourselves. We need not spread this story further.

Fifteen days later, they are alerted to a crowd gathering in the Meso- and Neolithic exhibit. There are, in this exhibit, flints and blades and tiny scale models of the houses, made from willow and shit, that would have dotted the landscape in the Neolithic period, and even tinier models of the round huts that they would have seen before. There are plastic replicas of some of the fish that are meant to swim in these waters, and the hazelnuts, and the lotus flower seeds, that were gathered and eaten. There are some of the dry fragmented bones of a woman, labelled as between eighteen and twenty years old, buried with numerous items, shown around her, and her three-to-five-month-old baby, and there are, for the first time, flowers on top of the casing which encloses them. There is a large bouquet of red roses, the plastic wrapping which held the name of the florist's removed, and then a second bouquet, of white roses and gypsophila; smaller, giving the impression of having been bought separately. The visitors stand around, look at the flowers, look at the staff, wait for someone to explain why they are there. Sinéad lifts the bouquets, says something inane like, aren't people so forgetful these days? Someone will be coming back for these!

He cringes. Yet he has nothing better to say.

Yusuf calls a meeting. He stands at the front of the room by a large whiteboard and speaks for about ninety seconds, outlining with incredible brevity the two discoveries of which he is aware: M-U-M, and the bouquets. Yusuf turns to the whiteboard and draws, in green ink, an enormous question mark.

We do not need this kind of publicity, Yusuf says. I am going to put more security at the front doors. Nobody comes in with flowers. Nobody comes in with anything they can't explain. Brian is going to scour the CCTV. Brian is going to find the perpetrator we know has already been active and we are going to think carefully about things like damage, criminal damage.

Naively, Yusuf does not say anything about the publicity which, inevitably, has already been attracted. Visitors have taken pictures of the bouquets and, twice, the museum has been tweeted at, asked for a response. Naomi, in charge of the museum's social media accounts, replies saying that it is great the visitors had a memorable time at the museum! Thanks for sharing images!

Then she contacts Yusuf.

Yes, they are feeling panicked. They are feeling scrutinised, vaguely hunted. Security guards at the front doors begin asking to see inside bags, which the population of the city take badly. Privately, when Yusuf calls in to Brian with coffee to see if anyone has been identified from the CCTV footage of the exhibits targeted, Yusuf admits feelings of great trepidation. Something is coming, says Yusuf. Brian pretends not to hear.

On opening up, security guards find carnations and a small white teddy left in the Neolithic section. There are sunflowers left in the Egyptian exhibit and there are more of the words, more of the notes, taped to the sides of the glass box in which her small face lies, exposed. The boards around the room inform anyone who can read that this is the body of a twenty-six-year-old woman who, the museum staff know from their investigations, lived in the North of Africa, gave birth at least once and who died in the agony of tuberculosis. The pieces of paper taped to the glass display box with pieces of Vincent Van Gogh Washi tape say on one side: YOU TOOK ME FROM MY BABY, and on the other: I AM SOMEBODY'S CHILD.

LET THEM REST

He says to the psychic, I feel worse now I'm seeing you, not better.

Yeah, says the psychic.

The psychic has asked about feelings of shame. We're starting miles away from the starting point with you, mate, they've said. We're trying to scrabble back up with you to even get at the question. It's—what you want—it's all covered over with these other dark things.

Right, he says. He makes an effort to slow himself down. He says things like: well, now, things like: let me think. He does not like to admit that the one word, SHAME, is enough, that there'd be things spilling out of his eyes had he not them closed. This feels worse, he wants to say, but he can't.

He's at the wedding of a relation in Cavan. He is wearing a navy-blue suit. The hotel has long flat gardens with circular flower-beds and gardeners planting, even as the wedding is ongoing, new bedding plants into the dry light soil. He watches guests, the bride, move through the garden, sweeping past the men with trowels, men on their knees. He joins a crowd at the bar, joins the conversation of the cousins he knows best discussing their mortgages, their marriages, and he has a cousin, Anna, dear gold earrings clutching at her ears, who says that she and her husband, well, you know, it's been almost five years, and they, you know, doesn't everyone, don't we all, she says, we want children but it's not, it's just not going to plan. She has the small sweet face of a moisturiser advert. Another cousin takes her hand. We've done the two cycles of IVF, Anna says, and it's, well, we just, we don't know what to do. In the silence, he clears his throat and suggests adoption, as he realises that nobody else will say the word in front of him.

Well, Anna says. She and the other cousins look at each other. Obviously for you, with you, it's been, it's been different but I suppose we wouldn't, I mean, after everything with your sister, we wouldn't want—

She looks at him, her eyes widened, her expression pleading. Don't make me say it, her face is saying. So he holds his hands up, in a don't-I-know-it gesture. Say no more, he says, O, I get you, alright.

Anna's face lights up with sweet, bright relief. She loves him, he can see it, she loves him for having understood, for having let there be no awkwardness. The cousins talk again of their families, their voices quick and heavy with meaning, and he knows he is being included as he has never been before. In a sense, he knows that this is it: real, true acceptance; that he has finally made it into the inner circle of which he has always been aware, that he has finally heard what they have always thought. This is how they speak of his sister. He hears them make the differentiation: he is one of them, his sister is not. Youse were always so different, the cousins say. Said quickly, implied through voices heavy with meaning: you worked, she didn't.

After the food, he steps outside, sits on a bench where there is paving.

His parents are somewhere inside the large dining area and he speaks to them only on arriving and as early as he can go, plants a kiss quickly on the powder and dry skin of his mother's cheek.

She's changed her name, he tells the psychic. She calls herself Opal. She told me, every story I ever wrote's about someone called Opal. And I said, the fuck are you on about, stories? What have you ever written?

He gets a job at the museum and he is proud of it and he asks her to meet him there, so they can have tea at the café downstairs where there are floor-to-ceiling windows. She is five years younger than him. She is sixteen. He is proud of the building, proud of the light, proud of the seats he saves them, with a plug for her to charge her phone and views of the trees, of the sculptures outside. He buys them scones and coffees and he brings them down to the table and he cuts open both scones, ready to serve, and he sees that the bursts of colour he's thought are berries, bursts of dark red-pink, purple-black, are just places where the dough's been stained with food dye. Well, he's livid about it. He's so angry he thinks he might cry. He goes up to the counter and he says, did you do this? Why did you do this? I'm going to the museum manager about this, right, because this is lying, this is cheating people out of their money, look at the state of this, look at the fucking state of this. At the time, he feels right, he feels justified. He even feels impressed with himself, at the volume of his voice, at the confidence he feels in challenging the man, challenging the system. But now he tends to remember only the slouch of his sister as he finally returns to their table, her long, long dark hair hanging down one side, her face buried into her elbow. She's put her head down on the café table, waiting, waiting, waiting for him to come back.

WHEN THIS PERSON DIED, PEOPLE CRIED AND CRIED

He is called to Yusuf's meetings with increasing frequency. The atmosphere in the room is bad. There have been candles left lit at the remains of the head of the Viking, and a non-denominational memorial card. There have been flowers, and notes, left at each of the three displays. At the Meso- and Neolithic displays, one card did cause upset even among some members of staff, one card which said: THIS IS A DEAD BABY.

When Sinéad is interviewed for the local news, instructed to show confusion and an expression of being genuinely disturbed by the goings-on, she references this note and says, I mean, it just shows the mindset of whoever is doing this, trying to be distasteful, trying to really shock and upset.

Isn't the truth of the matter, though, says the news reporter, that this is in fact a display of a dead baby?

The entire exchange makes it onto the six o'clock news.

At the meeting, Yusuf says he is going to hand over to Naomi. Many staff have probably already seen the latest development, but this is for the benefit of those who have not. Naomi begins with an overview of how difficult she has been finding her job lately, the amount of publicity and messages the museum's social media accounts have been receiving. I am struggling, she says, her voice cracking, with the implication that by working here, we are doing something wrong! She receives a light smattering of clapping.

Yusuf indicates, with his head, that the pace should be picked up.

There is a petition, Naomi says, that went live twenty-seven hours ago. It's, I can't believe I'm even saying this, it's a petition to get museum staff to sign up to donate our bodies on our deaths. It says that the people working at a museum which displays bodies should have to sign up to donate their bodies for display. And that if we don't want to do that, then we don't have the right to display other people.

The atmosphere in the room is sickening.

Naomi says, I'm really sorry to say that I think it's going to pick up steam. It's been live twenty-seven hours and already there've been three-hundred-and-fifty-seven signatures. That's not a lot, not in the grand scheme of things, but for the time scale and with the protests, sorry, I know you said, Yusuf, not to use that word, I mean the flowers and the notes and everything here, I think we should expect this to be picked up. I think we should definitely expect it to make the news again, even, and I think we need to think about how to be, sorry, Sinéad, more prepared for that when it comes.

Yusuf asks Naomi to repeat that last, and then writes, with a green pen, the number 357 on the mobile whiteboard. In a way, this is good news, folks! Yusuf says. I have asked Brian whether we can trace whoever started the petition. This is their first mistake. They have always been covered, okay, we have been unable to track them via the CCTV images, but with this website, we will have details, we will have an email address. We will be able to go to someone, to say, look at this, isn't this harassment?

Perhaps Yusuf also expects a small smattering of applause but there is none.

There is a white shroud in the Egyptian room, entirely covering the case with the mummy. There are huge white lilies laid out on the floor of the entire room, such that visitors do not enter, but stand at the archway which forms the entrance and stare. The cleaners are sent to clear the space and they report back that some people heckle them. Some boo, and some start a slow, sarcastic clap as the cleaners bend to lift the flowers. They return to tell Yusuf about it with the lilies' pollen all over their uniforms. They have it, orange, on their fingers, and on their cheeks from pushing fallen hair back behind their ears.

I AM SO TIRED

He meets his sister when he is seven years old and she is three. They look different: he is swarthy, his eyes dark, but her eyes are darker, her hair is actually, completely, black, and her skin is lighter only on the palms of her hands and the soles of her feet. Where do you come from? the psychic asks him. It is a question with which the psychic usually encourages poetic answers. I come from scraping the mould off my grandmother's jam, people say. I come from falling asleep in the wet warmth of a mobile classroom. I come from the river which runs through the bottom of the town, in which my uncle fell and drowned one stag-night. He tries this, at first. He comes from sitting with his sister, trying to read their parents' expressions. He comes from repeated nightmares that he is an animal, not living but held hostage in a body, an animal like a pet rabbit, held somewhere cold and lonely for years until death; repeated nightmares that he is one of those animals impregnated, birthed, only to be chopped up and fed to those other animals that are preferred.

But eventually he says, they adopted us from Russia. There is, he feels, no way for these words to convey the magnitude of what happened. He has, he tells the psychic, at fifteen he has a small breakdown, a shutdown of sorts, on realising the number of ethnic groups in Russia, that Russia was not an answer but just the beginning of a question, that it holds one-hundred-and-forty-seven-million people, one-hundred-and-ninety ethnic groups, millions of Indigenous people, all of their cultures, all of their religions, all of these histories. He has this minor breakdown, he starts, he says, he dreams, how will they find me?

He comes from his parents. They send out round robins at Christmas, even now, reporting on weekend breaks or a slightly longer cycle, and they send them out through all the years of their growing up, they send pictures of his sister with a caption, in italics, *SHE IS LIKE A DOLL! SERIOUSLY!!!* They say, DIMPLES LIKE DADDY. They say, OUR BARBIE-GIRL! She grows through the pictures, she is seven, ten, thirteen. Here she is, winning prizes. WHAT A LAMB!

You think they didn't see you as people, says the psychic.

They only love her when she is small, when she looks how they want. They don't love her, they've just dropped her, because she turns out to be a person, not just this image, because she wants things and she knows things and she likes things and they never wanted that. They never think about how it is to be us, he says. They just think, they want a baby, they get a baby. I didn't even know half of Russia is Asia, he says. How does that happen? We didn't even know that we're Asian.

He can't remember meeting her but there's a photo, his sister in a red onesie and a Russian-style hat, a circle of fake fur, and he doesn't know, even now, if their parents bought it as a joke or if they thought it'd be enough of a culture. He comes from that day, anyway, comes from seeing himself in the darks of her eyes.

I want to say something, says the psychic. There is, of course, grief here. There is, obviously, loss. You were born and you don't know exactly where, exactly to whom. But I'd like to suggest that maybe you'd've always been like this. Maybe this just is who you are. Maybe you'd've always been anxious. Maybe you'd've always been this kind of questioning person. Maybe you'd've always felt the need to squash yourself down, to do what you have to do to please. There could be a tendency, maybe, to attribute too much to your origins here. People come to me, O my god, legions come to me and they've lived their whole lives with biological families, they've had a weird time but they've no unbelievable traumas, these people come and they sit and they say: I need help. I don't know who I am. There's no reason for them not to know, you know? But they sit there and that's their question, that's what they're saying, who am I?

What do you tell them? he asks.

Well, it depends, the psychic says. Really, it has to depend on the person.

RESPECT YOUR ELDERS

He sees the clip himself, before the meeting with Yusuf's whiteboard and its intermittent count of the signatures on the museum-staff petition, before Brian stands up and announces the Five New Cardinal Rules for Spotting a Disrupter on the Premises, before the debate on closing the exhibits, before it's announced that Naomi's gone off on the sick.

The reporter doesn't show their face, and they are identified only as a local resident, but still he knows their voice immediately, knows the rhythm with which they pause for breath. After a slideshow, a montage, of the images which visitors take and share online, as well as footage the reporters themselves have managed to record of cushions left at each of the three displays of human remains with the words, ALWAYS IN OUR HEARTS, come clips of conversation with people they stop on the street.

Have you seen the protests? the reporter says.

I have. I have to be honest, I've visited the museum potentially hundreds of times. I was taken here as a child, I have come back as an adult. Until all of this started, I never considered, I never thought about what we had here. It's been, I would say, there has been an awakening. I've seen some talk on Twitter coming from the left, people taking this view of, why all this fuss about the dead? Focus on the living! Where are, I've seen words to this effect, where are the protests for this living person? Where are the protests for this living thing? Because there is, you know, there is so much disrespect towards currently living humans. But I would just say, I would counter that first of all, we don't know who's behind this protest, so we can't say that they're not doing both. That's the first thing. But even if all their attention is on this currently, I mean, they feed into each other, right? That's the second thing. These, they are, we're all connected. We cannot say that the display of the remains of, let's be honest, predominantly people of colour in institutions run by mostly white people, in this country at least, is definitely not contributing to the ill-treatment of people of colour. I think it's absolutely fair to assume that it contributes, even in a subconscious way, to our dehumanisation, to the disrespect we often experience. And, you know, that's a word that's come up again and again in this protest: RESPECT. And it's worth asking ourselves: what is it doing, to send our kids in to have them look at these people, at these dead people, without any mourning rites, without prayer, without songs, without ritual? Is this, is this what we want? We don't have to agree on, we don't even have to have, a religion, a god, I think we're forgetting, we're killing what's in ourselves as the basics, you know? That we pray, we respect, that living is sacred, that the body is sacred, that what's left is sacred. Death is holy. This iPad kid goes in and he's taking pictures of a dead North African woman. What are we killing, then, in the children? You wouldn't want, you wouldn't put, your aunt on display and we can say, too recent, no, that's too recent, but it doesn't really matter, you wouldn't want anyone you love on display, you would fight that, we know it. So if it's about love, then why don't we love these people? Because we don't know them, they don't deserve these same rights? These people lived, they died, people buried them, begged that they would know peace.

Well, says the reporter. This is Melanie McAreavy, reporting for—

They haven't gone anywhere, says the interviewee. Every one is still here.

Somebody puts the clip on Twitter. The clip does very, very well. At the meeting, Brian describes it as The Latest Development. Yusuf sounds, at times, close to tears. Lawyers from a large London museum have been in touch and offered to help them draft a statement and come up with a Game Plan for the coming weeks.

YOU DESTROYED THEIR GRAVE

He sees her when she is nineteen. She comes to his flat and she is supposed to stay for two nights. He is excited to take her out, to buy her nice meals, to show what he has got for himself with this good museum job, to be good to her, to show her that he respects the distance she has put between herself and their parents, that they can, she and him, be just siblings, that they do not need the others. She has tattoos on her shoulders which are bandaged, still healing. They go to a restaurant and even before the waiter has come with menus she suggests playing cards and it wounds him, for some reason, wounds him that he is already unable to sustain her attention and he reacts, he over-reacts, he says, For god's sake, can he not have five fucking minutes, and she looks uncomfortable, then, and he is sorry, so sorry, but he doesn't quite say it. They order and he eats everything, takes a dessert, then a coffee, because he refuses to admit that he's fucked it up, that the night is bad, and he says they can take a taxi home but she says she wants to walk it. They are almost the same height, walking past the park which backs onto the museum where he works. She is quiet and it is cold. He says, what are you thinking about?

She has one memory, she says. It lives extremely far back in her head, buried far under the weight of all the days there have been since, everything their parents did, everything, all of it, and she sees it only when she is half-waking, lying down, staring at the backs of her eyelids, only when it is quiet enough, only when everything is quite right. They are in a car but she is not in a baby-seat, not wearing a seat-belt, she is wrapped and held close to someone's body, and they are in the passenger seat of the car, her and the woman, and somebody else is driving, and the woman bends her head low to say things which are not in English, and she, she is pretending to sleep though she is not sleeping, she is listening, and they stop at a place where there is water, and across the water, somewhere in the distance, there is fire, there is fire.

Well, he remembers that, he says. That happened here. It was a cousin of their mother's was over, a cousin who had moved, who lives, still, he believes, in Portugal, who came over with his partner and they babysat one night, and she was three, and he was eight, and on the news this cousin saw that there was fire in hills, fire on the mountains, that farmers had been burning gorse and lost all control, and he wanted to see it, the cousin, and he put them all out in the car, and they drove and they watched it, some of the burning.

He doesn't, he didn't, he doesn't understand what he's doing until it's done, there's nothing, he can't do anything, he can't take it back, he can't change it, and they're walking, they walk, they walk back to his flat, and what he's done, he can't change it, he can't undo it, and she stays, she stays one day, she stays one night, and they say goodbye and he says, Listen, he says to her, you're always welcome here, you know that, you can stay anytime.

The psychic says, you have your question.

Yes.

He says, is it her?

That's not how it works, says the psychic. The protest is not one person, it is multiple people, it's not organised, it's spontaneous, the museum can't track the people because it's never the same people. The handwriting, the pens, the paper, it's not traceable because they are all, always, different.

You're worried that it's her, says the psychic. You're worried that she's angry, that she's trying to get at you, somehow. But you're more worried that it's not her.

Where is she? he says.

Is she alive? he says.

The psychic puts their hands up, fingers splayed. I don't do missing people, mate. I should have said that at the start.

SAY A PRAYER

The team at the museum would like to reassure the public that we are, first and foremost, a resource for the community. Our primary goal is always education through, restoration of, and care for our artefacts. With the passage of time, we continually review which of the items entrusted to us are actively on display and also remove other items for storage. We recognise the current level of concern created by some of our displays, in particular that of the Egyptian mummy, our display of remains found at a Neolithic site in Westmeath, and other artefacts sourced from various locations, including a skull from outside Bergen in Norway. The museum team are currently reviewing displays with a view to altering those for the coming year, and some of these may be moved to storage. However, the museum at all times retains the right to display these artefacts again at a later date; this remains, and will always remain, at the discretion of museum staff.

Novena

I

The flying ants are everywhere. At a certain time of the day, at a certain time of the year, they are there when he tries to open the van's door, there falling down onto the seat. Felix has a brother-in-law who has eaten such ants. The brother-in-law catches them with his hands and with a net and Felix has a text from him this morning: *Tough day for you mate tough news.* Felix hasn't replied. The text is from his sister, really. There are flying ants walking across the dashboard. It's that time of year.

He gets breakfast at the market once he's set up. He likes to. He likes to pick up a bun, pick up a coffee, and sit at his stand saying, 'This isn't so bad, is it?' He likes the feeling it gives him: walking around, knowing people. When he heard there was a new bakery stand coming, two men, a married couple, he really thought about what he'd open with. He said, in the end, 'Sure, it's just wee buns, isn't it?' And then he said, 'Ha-ha, I'm sure youse're sick hearing that one.' And then he said, 'I'm Felix, I've the antiques stall.' And he called it antiques, though the term was a catch-all; he sold things that looked old. A one-man car-boot sale, his wife had said, when she loved him.

He orders a coffee at Tara's stall and she says Moll will bring it over. He likes this: being known. He has brass candlesticks, paper-weights, a mounted piece of fool's gold. The girl comes over with the drink. The lid is compostable; that's what the lid says.

'Thanks, kid,' says Felix. He asks her to wait a second. He says, 'I'm wondering, what do you think of this lay-out?' It is early but Felix is always like this, a sociable person. 'Product-wise, I'm wondering, does anything jump out?'

The girl looks at the paper-weights. She looks at a picture of the Sacred Heart. She looks at Felix and she shrugs with a discomfort that he does not read.

'What do you think of the pictures?' Felix asks her. He points at a set of watercolours: desert scenes, swathes of sand and sky. 'Do you know that part of the world?'

There's something not right with his tone as he asks it. He regrets it as soon as it's said.

Moll looks at him. 'I'm from here,' she says.

Felix is mortified.

'I know that,' he says. 'That's not what I meant.'

He sits down when she's gone. He takes the lid off the coffee. When he checks his phone, there is a message from his sister: *Hope B is OK.*

This message fucks him right off. His sister is mad for the drama, that's why she's messaging. There's no other reason to text.

Leave me alone.

He wants to message that back.

I'm at work. I can't be at this.

He has it typed, but he doesn't send it. It's Saturday morning, and the market's filling up. He reads what she sent again and again.

How the fuck would I know? he types. *I don't even know where she is.*

II

Tara spends many hours of her life on her phone. It would disturb her to think just how many hours, so she doesn't. If someone had her phone, they could know more about her than any person ever has. The phone is not separate from Tara. It is an extension of her. It remembers things better than she does, suggests words in the patterns she uses them; it knows her thoughts. She is there, in the screenshots she takes, in the Notes that she makes.

She maintains two Instagram accounts: one using her name, followed by and following people from school, from various jobs. She posts stories relating to her stall, what hours she'll be at the market, and posts pictures of herself only occasionally, maybe once every three months, when she looks very happy. She has a second account on which she follows the accounts she actually wants to. Things are harmless but this is it: she is still scared that other people might see. On this account, Tara follows a lot of Mormon women, beautiful people with seven, eight children for whom they sew dresses and make from-scratch sourdough bread.

Things are split. Tara works at a call centre, but there is her life, and then there is the image of her life; she does not disclose the call centre on the Instagram account. Each week at the market, she takes a photo of the stall all set up, her pastel take-away cups, and shares it. She writes things like: coffee BEANS, one of your five-a-day?! She staggers posts throughout the week, vaguely giving the impression that she's working at it full-time. When she meets people, she talks about the stall. They bring it up, because they've seen it. It looks right. It looks good. There she is, twenty-six, with the help of a teenager because business is just going that well. She doesn't ever, directly, lie.

Moll works on the weekends; she got the job in a manner that left Tara the last to find out. Tara came home and her mother relayed the conversation she'd had with Rita, Moll's grandmother, with the confidence of someone who had given complete assurances, and Tara understood that she was being informed rather than asked; that, in fact, the arrangement had been made. She gives Moll twenty pounds a day. She does not need the help and she notices the money, but she has enjoyed being able to say, sometimes, that she's nipping out for a smoke break. Tara doesn't smoke, but it lets her stand outside on her phone.

She stands outside. On her phone, a Mormon woman is milking a cow by hand. There is the sound of milk hitting the bucket, the small warm words of children weaving in and out around them. There is an enormous dog, a toddler clinging to its yellow fur.

There are so many of them, these families.

Tara spends months, spends years, of her life like this: watching. These Mormons, these women, they feed their children raw milk. They film their children galloping on horses with no helmets, no saddle; let them run, unattended, through huge farms and fields. They follow none of the rules in which Tara believes. But nothing bad ever happens to them. She's unsure when but she realised, at some point, that the world is like this: some people have seven children and all of them live.

III

Moll's mother tells people that her mother lives with them, but this is not the truth: they live with Moll's grandmother. Moll's mother is a social worker. She works unhealthy hours, under extreme stress. Moll says that her mother turns everything into a negative. 'Isn't this nice?' someone might say to her, enjoying meeting up. 'If only,' Moll's mother will say, 'if only we'd done it before.'

Her dad is in Derry. She sees him often but has never lived there. Her dad's parents brought him to Dungannon from East Timor when he was a baby, some time between walking and school; he's lived in Derry since university. She used to stay with him every weekend but now it's less regimented, it's more when she fancies. Moll tells people that as a child she thought herself funny—every talent show, every drama class, she was up there, trying—and took years to realise that her father killed himself laughing only because he loved her. There he was: eyes-closed, knees-weak, thigh-slapping laughing.

She's woken by her grandmother, who comes into her bedroom, opens the curtains, pulls her duvet away, saying always, 'Molly?' with that tone: expectation. She takes a small backpack and she walks up the road. She's learning to drive, something her grandmother and mother are paying for. They got her insured on the car and gave her L-plates for her birthday. When she's in Derry, her dad takes her to a car-park and they practise bay-parking. At home, she does one lesson a week. People are invested in the learning. 'You'll have so much freedom,' they say. They seem so certain.

She looked at Tara's Instagram account before she started working for Tara at the stall. It was a little embarrassing.

Tara says, unironically, Reunited and it feels so good! She uses crying-laughing emojis. She shows Moll what photos she is planning to post before she posts them. 'Got them all up so everyone knows how much fun I'm having!' she says, as though—as though she knows it is strange, as though she is self-aware, but she can't stop feeding into it, trying to make others jealous.

It's difficult not to believe that a person has always been exactly how you find them. Here Tara is, Moll thinks: someone who has always pretended to smoke, someone who has always been bleaching their darker hair blonde, someone who has always kept her bank-card, cash and ID in the fractured pink plastic of her phone case.

The first day that Moll worked at the market, she and Tara started to walk home together, and as they walked a group of boys cycled past them. 'O god,' Tara said, 'I hope there's not any trouble.' She was serious, beginning to walk at a speed she would obviously struggle to maintain. 'There's my cousin,' said Moll. She waved at him going past. 'They're, like, thirteen.'

Sometimes she lies and says she has to leave a few minutes early, or hang around a bit late, to avoid that walk home together. It just depresses her, listening.

A woman is buying an amber necklace. Felix doesn't know if the amber is real or not; he has it priced as though it is, and the woman doesn't ask. She haggles; he lets her feel that she's beaten him down a fiver. He puts it in a little gift bag for her. She's excited by the purchase. 'There's good coffee,' he says, 'at that stall down there.' He points at Tara. Tara sees him, waves.

The day is going slow enough. When there is a breeze

he sees some of them: flying ants. In the toilet he hears the local news headlines on the cleaner's wireless radio and it upsets him. He stands at the urinal feeling unsteady. The documentary programme set to be released this evening is unequivocal in its findings: the fertility clinic based in the city has conned an unknown number of patients out of thousands of pounds. The investigation has found that—

There are Americans over for an Irish-dancing competition. They have hoodies with Celtic crosses and spirals on. 'Have you anything with leprechauns?' ask two women. They aren't even embarrassed. 'No,' Felix says. 'I've just got what you see here.'

'We've been looking all morning,' says one woman. 'I just don't understand why nobody has leprechauns here.'

Felix shrugs. 'That's life,' he says. It doesn't make sense.

He remembers his wife on an IV drip in that fertility clinic. They gave her steroids. She had prescriptions. That woman, pale hair and sweet pink nails, she guaranteed his wife a baby. She said that nothing was out of the question. It was all within reach.

They borrowed money from everyone.

He scratches the back of his neck. He stands at his stall. He takes out his phone, looks at the message from his sister. They loaned him thousands, to be fair, his sister and his brother-in-law. They borrowed money from everyone, his wife's family, some of their friends. Everyone struggled.

He thinks of everyone they took money from seeing those headlines.

It was a con. The clinic was fake.

They had her on drips, on steroids, on medications, and not one person in the clinic had any medical training. Some English doctor was sending them over signed blank prescriptions; that was how they got what they wanted. She could have died. They didn't know what the fuck they were doing.

He wanted to stop years before she did. It hurt him, that it hadn't worked, but he was still confident that they would survive it. They were a family on their own, just the two of them, whatever happened, they were enough as they were. He was saying these things for years. And then he said he would leave for months before he did. He said he would. It had been seven years. They didn't have lives outside of it, that was how it felt. It had to stop. He said it over and over. But she wouldn't listen. She was obsessed. And he did think of it as something like an addiction. He did think of it as something like a disease. And when they separated, it was just—he needed time, he needed space—he wanted his wife, but the wife he'd had before she only wanted his baby. He only dated casually. He only dated to show his wife that he was serious: if she didn't stop, he would do it, he would really leave, he would really find someone else; that was all that he wanted. And he was going out, he was seeing people, and he thought at the time, he thought, he was serious and he had to be serious and it would be over soon, and he could have her back.

And then this woman he'd seen got back to him.

She was pregnant. She was having his child.

IV

Tara is serving the couple Moll says asked her for some special kind of sweetener, which they don't have. Americans in person are different from those Tara watches; in person, she finds herself uneasy. Moll says, 'They say genocidal things.'

'You wouldn't get this for that in the States!' one says to the others, raising her disposable cup. 'Ha-ha!' says Tara. What choice does she have?

When they leave, Moll says, wiping down the end of the counter where Tara has laid out a shaker of cinnamon and a shaker of cocoa powder: 'Everyone's talking about that fertility clinic.'

Tara doesn't know what Moll's talking about. Moll repeats herself. It's a big clinic. People have been going for decades, paying thousands upon thousands of pounds. And it was fake. It was a scam.

She says to Moll, 'I'm going to head out for a smoke-break.' Moll nods. Tara stands out by the bins, where the sun is warm on her when she's stood still in it. She takes out her phone and squints at the screen. She finds Instagram. She can just about see one of the Mormon women hanging washing on a line. Tara relaxes. Her breathing slows. She watches. There is light coming through the fabric as it sways where it's hung. There's a baby in the basket, watching its mother, raising its hands. The woman is in a dress which moves in the breeze. She steps around the basket, hanging the washing. Other children run in and out; it's impossible to tell how many.

Tara feels, when she thinks of it, a strong dread at the thought of finishing the day at the market, of having to return home. She lives with her parents. She's whitened the walls of her deep pink bedroom but it's still absolutely recognisable: the same bed that she sleeps in, the same houses she sees when she looks out the window. It's the same tarmac, the same pylons.

On her phone, the woman's kitchen is wooden and the table is dusted with flour. She turns out bread-dough and begins to knead.

Her parents label certain things in the fridge: *saving this for a recipe. pls do not touch*. They cook together, work their way through entire cookbooks one page at a time. They get in together, leave the house together. They met as traffic wardens watching the same corner. Tara lies on her back, on her stomach, spends hours on the phone that shows her the lives of other people. She works and she works. She splashes through dirty water, pooled on the pavement, on her way to the bus-stop; she comes the same way back. She has tried to remember who she was as a child. She has flashes of it. She vaguely remembers passions, ardent beliefs; her school had a poster in the RE rooms that said, lose yourself in the service of others, and Tara truly believed she would do it. She pictured herself noble and good and exhausted. She would perform surgeries. She would teach. She'd give everything she had and then gather up the scrapings to give those away too. She feels that, sleeping in her childhood bedroom: some sense of separateness; some sense of guilt.

She can't remember not being aware of the other children, of the other babies. She once read in a magazine about how, at different times, graveyards were places where people had picnics, places of, at times, happiness, and inspiration, and she wished, with a fervour, with a sense of irritation, that she could have had that. Because the other children have a presence, even when it's not acknowledged. And maybe it could have been easier. What she remembers—she remembers—it was public. Her parents spoke about trying, and treatments. Her mother was on the prenatal vitamins, had a hand raised in refusal at any talk of drink, and people knew, people were excited, and then when it went wrong, there was this constant, staggered distress. They were meeting people for months afterwards, people who said, O god, they hadn't known—such a shame, such a shame. It happened everywhere. O no! people said. Eyes watered. Her parents stood there, together. It was like that. It's so easy to announce a pregnancy, her mother said, but there's no real way to take it back. Her parents stood there. They always had this hope. They always had this burning devastation. Tara was only a child. She was there, but she wasn't. They were separate.

She couldn't say it. She couldn't word it. What would we have had if you hadn't needed more? It was a tragedy for them, that they had only Tara. It was, in ways, their defining grief.

She remembers standing between her parents, behind. She remembers walking ahead, the two of them in-step together. Am I not a baby? She might've said it.

She puts her phone away when she hears people coming: voices, talking. 'Fuck me,' one of them says. 'That coffee is bitter as god.'

V

Moll is trying to be more blunt. She has realised that the way she speaks focuses, to an extreme degree, on the comfort of the person to whom she is speaking. She is trying to say what she wants to. She is trying to order food without saying, could I, please, if you don't mind, thank you, if that's no bother, if it's not hassling you, cheers. Her dad was saying to her, when he saw her interact at a restaurant, 'It's called an order for a reason, love. You're supposed to say what you want.'

Tara's made them both a mocha; things are winding down. The tourists have gone and the people dandering around now are not buying drinks. So Moll says: 'Can I head on early?' And Tara's face registers surprise but she still says, immediately, 'Sure.' Before Moll goes, she asks her to help her make a boomerang of two pastel coffee-cups hitting each other in a cheers. She puts it on Instagram. Over the image, in glowing letters, she puts: livin' la vida mocha!

As Moll's walking home she gets a call from her driving instructor: he wants to move her lesson from Tuesday to Thursday. Also, he says, his prices have gone up. He has to match the price of petrol, he says.

'Well, I'll have to see about that,' Moll says. There is a silence on the line. But she's pleased with herself for saying it. She says, 'I'm a teenager, Richard. There is, like, a spending cap.'

When she gets home from a driving lesson, her mother, her grandmother ask how it was. In the beginning, Moll answered honestly but this only annoyed them. They want to hear that she's progressing, even if she's not. They're confusing like that.

Well, she's pleased with herself, that day. She imagines telling her dad about the conversation. 'And I says to him, dad: "Richard, I'm a teenager."' She knows he'll be pleased. She's sweating a little when she reaches the house. Moll's mother's in the kitchen, at the table. Her grandmother's at the sink. It's quiet. Her mother is picking at her hands. She says something about someone from her work: she used to visit the family, and a woman would be on at her to sell her hair, but now it's only the man, a man who begs her to tell him who he is.

It upsets Moll. The image attacks her, violently. 'Well, he's just sat there, isn't he,' her mother says, 'going, tell us, tell us who I am.' Moll snaps, 'I thought it was supposed to be confidential!'

Her mother says, although she's heard, her mother says: 'What?'

'It's supposed to be confidential,' Moll says. 'You're not supposed to talk about people!'

'Do you think I need this?' her mother says. She stands up. 'I've had it up to here with this shit, Molly. I am sick of walking on eggshells around you!'

Moll's grandmother says, 'Girls!'

'As if you are ever here,' Moll says. 'As if you are ever around me.'

Her grandmother is there, between them. 'Girls! Girls!'

On their lessons, Richard the driving instructor often makes Moll pull over. 'What was that about?' he asks Moll, and Moll says, 'What?' Richard's hands are dry with psoriasis and his nails are very short. 'You do,' he says, 'what we call in the business: unexplainable things. You do things that I can't—I don't know what you're doing.' He reaches his hands out to the dashboard. 'Why would you do that, Molly? I'm not—I just, listen, that was dangerous back there. I need to know what you're thinking. You should be better than this.'

Moll says, 'I don't know what I'm doing!' Moll says, 'I'm trying my best!'

The driving instructor says, 'You're looking at the wrong side of the road!'

Often he is so flustered he calls her by the wrong name. 'Jesus Christ, Milly!' He's yelled that before. 'Hello?' he says, 'Mel, is there anyone home?'

VI

Felix and his wife are still married. He doesn't know where she is.

Her family, initially devastated but understanding of the separation, said they were sickened by his behaviour when he told them, he had to tell them, that he was having a baby. He hasn't heard from them in years. He posts pictures of his stall, of the market, on Facebook.

It'd be nice if one of them would message. He knew them so well.

You're good?

They could say it.

The baby was born. She was healthy. He and the baby's mother were never even together but he tried to be there, he tried to be helpful. She got a new boyfriend. She didn't want his visits. She said he could see the baby once a month.

He was aware—he's still aware—that it's nothing like a fair split but in ways he feels, he's always felt, that he doesn't deserve the child anyway.

She's seven now. They are different, Felix and his child's mother, it is in the little things; when he sees her, little things disturb him. He picked her up once when she was three and she'd her nails painted, her curly hair straightened. He thought he saw mascara.

'Did you do that?' he asked her mother.

It was for a family party, her mother explained. Something in her partner's family.

They came to the market once. It was Felix's idea; he thought it'd be nice for his daughter to see how he worked. It was around Halloween. She came with her mother, her mother's partner. She was dressed in an outfit from *Grease*. When he saw her, Felix thought: this has all gone wrong.

'Why's she dressed like that?' he asked her mother. He could feel himself blushing. 'She's six years old, what's she doing in, why's she dressed like that?'

'She loves it!' said her mother. 'She's just obsessed with *Grease*. I never thought she'd sit through it but she's sat there non-stop, she's obsessed.'

'You never let her watch *Grease*?' Felix said, his voice high and unsteady. 'She's six years old, you're never letting her watch *Grease*?'

He was annoying her mother. She let go of the child's hand. 'If you've got something to say to me, Felix, say it.'

But he didn't. He gave the child a vintage cardigan he'd been keeping, a crocheted one of real wool. The child passed it to her mother. She put it in her handbag.

The market is closing. People are packing up, covering their stalls with the white fabric, their shrouds. He sees Tara, the woman from the coffee stand, stood with her phone out, scrolling. He calls over to her on a whim, van keys in hand. 'Lift?' he says.

Tara nods.

It's a whim. His head's away, really. He's thinking: he needs to get that documentary set up to record. He knows the findings, he's heard the headlines on the local news all day, but he should see it. He should watch the whole thing. Maybe there'll be some website set up. Maybe there'll be some kind of support.

Out in the van, some of the ants are dead. Felix feels bad about that. He's startled by how strongly he feels regret. He should have left a window open. He could've, too; it would have cost him nothing.

There was a long time when Felix's sadness made his world almost uninhabitable. Everything he read—people had tortured some cat, its body had been found—Mike Tyson got into fighting because as a child he was bullied, because he had had to stand there as a child while someone tore the head off his pet—it was everything, it was everywhere, things were horrific. When the grief passed, his child was maybe thirteen months old. She'd said her first word. Mama, she said.

VII

At five o'clock, Moll's grandmother begins getting ready to leave the house for Mass. She gets her handbag ready. She changes her clothes. At half five, Moll's mother says that she'll run them up to the church in the car. It's a hot day. She says it'll be easier this way.

Moll sits in the back.

Moll's grandmother is always defensive when she sees how few cars are in the church carpark. She always feels the need to say something to Moll like, 'It'll fill up, just you see', or: 'That's all the people walking these days, people walk up, they don't drive.'

It doesn't matter to Moll. She doesn't care.

'I think you're hormonal,' Moll's grandmother is saying. 'I think that you're hormonal and you're both stressed. You're like cats.'

'Thanks,' Moll says.

Her mother parks in the carpark. As she and her grandmother move to get out, Moll's mother calls her back. 'Give me a minute,' she says. 'Moll, please.'

Moll looks at her grandmother, who nods her head at the car. Moll gets back in. She sits in the back. Her mother has her hands in her lap. At first, she doesn't speak. Moll watches her grandmother climb the steps to the church. 'She'd better save me a seat,' Moll says, though the church will be almost empty: she doesn't want her mother to know.

'I don't know why it's like this,' her mother says. The words are slow coming. 'I don't know if it's—I mean, I wonder, it's like—you've got mum, and you've got your dad. You don't need me.'

'This isn't fair,' Moll says. She leans forward between the seats. She says it exactly, exactly what she means. 'You're trying to make me feel guilty. You always do this. You want me to feel bad.'

'No,' her mother says, her voice light with a rising panic. 'No, no, no, that's not it. Look, now you're getting angry, this isn't what I want, Molly, I didn't want this. I want us to be friends, I don't know why it's so hard. I want us to be friends. I want us to know each other.'

The car is hot and the air is still.

'I'm going to be late,' Moll says. She moves to open the car door. Her mother locks it. 'What the fuck?' Moll says. She pulls on the car handle. 'Open the door!'

'Molly,' her mother says, as Moll shouts at her about the door, about opening the door. 'Listen to me, Molly. Molly,' she's screaming, 'I need you to listen.' She puts her head down, rests it against the steering wheel. 'I had this job,' she says. 'I was just out of school. I did stupid stuff. I did, like, foot rubs and hand massages and this kind of shit and I was told, when we were asked, we had to say that it helped, we said that it boosted blood flow, and it reduced stress, and that they wouldn't miscarry, you know, they were paying through the nose for this shit, for me and other stupid students, and everyone just lied to them, we all just lied to them.'

'At the clinic?' Moll says.

'I knew it wasn't right. But you were only a baby.'

'So it's my fault again,' Moll says.

'No!' her mother says, her voice red, cracking. 'It was mum. I told her. I knew what we were doing. But she told me not to say. She told me. She said I'd be blacklisted, she said I'd never work again. I was so worried. She told me all this stuff, Molly. She said, what if they took you away?'

Moll's chest, her torso, is tight. 'You're a social worker,' she says. 'You know nobody could've taken me away for that. For what, being a fucking whistle-blower?'

'I wasn't a social worker then,' her mother says. 'I wasn't doing that yet. I didn't know. I believed her. I didn't know anything.' She breathes heavily, her head still against the steering wheel. 'And then, I just left it. I don't know. I didn't do anything, even when I did know. It could've changed. I thought it would've changed.' Moll's mother isn't looking at her. 'I can't get it out of my head,' she says. 'It's—I don't even know how to say it. There's this evil, Molly.'

'You need to let me out of the car,' Moll says. She hears the doors click as they unlock. 'I don't understand why you're telling me this,' she says. 'It's nothing to do with me.' She can feel her mother looking at her, her face tight and desperate, but Moll watches only her own hand as it reaches for a handle, pushes the car door open.

'You were the making of me, Molly,' her mother says.

The church is quiet. The sermon is long. Children in the congregation are noticeable by their rarity. It has been written in the parish bulletin that they may not, going forward, have enough priests to do single funerals. In his homily, the priest says that the point of Mercy is that it is not Deserved. If Forgiveness is given and it is Deserved, then that is not Mercy but Justice. This is why Mercy is so powerful. This is why we beg for it. Forgive us, she feels the priest is saying. Please.

After communion, they sit listening to a CD of hymns playing through the speaker; there is no choir. Moll's grandmother's head falls on Moll's shoulder.

She snores.

VIII

His brother-in-law caught them five or six years ago. Felix was out the back of their house and he was there, scooping them off the garden wall, sweeping a net around to catch the ones flying. He called them alates. One day a year, winged queens take to the air. Many types of ant do it; termites, too. Felix stood and watched. His sister was still in work; she wouldn't be home a while. She wasn't home until the flying ants had been fried, their fat abdomens turned stripey. His brother-in-law said that they tasted like lemon.

'Cool,' Felix said. He was having a hard time. The baby was six, maybe seven months old.

'They're calling this the Great Dying, Felix,' his brother-in-law said. 'I'm not—I wouldn't be a prepper or anything, but I think we have to learn what we can before the internet's gone.'

When Felix's sister got home, she brought out drinks and sat with them in her work clothes, the high-waisted trousers and blouse.

It took hours and hours for the sky to darken.

When it did, his sister said, "Felix, you've done nothing wrong."

They'd had a few drinks. The baby was six, maybe seven months old.

He's heard terrible stories in the time since, sordid stories, men getting other women pregnant while their own wives are mid-IVF cycle or even mid-miscarriage. He's heard terrible stories but his is bad enough, he feels. He knows what his wife would say: he got a baby in the end.

Felix likes his brother-in-law. He speaks calmly. He's not religious. He knows a lot. Felix thinks his sister is good for his brother-in-law and vice versa, which is good. He can't think of many couples like that. They'd never wanted children, they both said that; they'd been nothing but good to Felix and his wife, all those years they were trying.

His brother-in-law got some of the ants by just letting them climb all over his hands.

When he stops in the street where Tara's directed him, Felix opens his own door as she climbs out the passenger side. He sweeps the insects, dead on the dashboard, into his palm. He holds them there. Tara is watching him. He doesn't know her. He leaves his door open and walks over to the small stretch of grass outside her house and lets them fall. He feels better, then, marginally: they'll go back to the earth. Maybe something will eat them. Some kind of bird.

In the car, Tara noticed there was a CD playing, though Felix turned the volume down to zero, so that they couldn't hear it. She could still see the tracks counting up. She thought about speaking to him. She thought about it the whole way. She felt that there were words solidifying in her mouth, clogging. I just thought I was going to be this bright person. She almost said it. I thought I would have all this energy. And I thought, I knew, my parents weren't happy but I thought I knew why and I thought I could avoid it, but I haven't, and maybe I can't. I always thought it was so grim the way people talked about getting older and I thought I'd never do that but then I am getting older and I do, I can't help it, because it's like, it's like, it's me who's exhausted, it's me doing these shifts, and I thought, I thought it would be different for us. I thought we were going to be these brilliant people. I thought the adults we knew were miserable but only because, I guess I thought they weren't doing it right. I thought because we didn't want to do it we would find a way to not have to but now I'm thinking, O my god, nobody has a fucking choice. And I thought I was going to have this beautiful life but I just, I just feel tired all the time, actually. Even when I'm only just waking, even, even I think when I am asleep, I think that I dream that I'm tired.

I think that I even dream it.

It's like that the whole way. She almost says it.

'Thanks for the lift,' she says, finally, out of the van. 'I usually walk with Molly, so don't worry, I'll not be begging one off you every week.'

'You're grand,' Felix says. He's looking at the house. He clears his throat. 'I'm wrecked. You know yourself. The stall barely wipes its face.' He says, clunkily, 'I'll see you the next day, kid.'

Tara waves him off.

She can't bring herself to go into the house.

She sits on the front step. The day is warm and the sun is strong. There are, in places, little insects, flying. Her parents will be inside. She stretches her legs out in front of her. In her head, there is this ringing, the sound that starts in her ear and floods into her head and has her collapse, has her always fainting.

She dated, for some years, an identical twin. In arguments, she always found herself yelling, 'You will never understand how lonely I feel!' It disturbed them both. 'What the fuck are you on about?' he'd say. 'I'm sorry, okay? I should have took the bins out.'

It thrummed in her head all the time she was with him.

They split up because she became consumed with this conviction, this knowing, that someone else would, absolutely, make him happier, that there was some better love out there for him. She was depriving him, this was what she believed, and she made herself unlikeable, disagreeable, until he realised exactly what she had always known; until he left.

Felix, she thought about saying in the car. I never had any doubt that I wasn't what they wanted. This was not their plan. They were always so clear that I wasn't enough.

It thrums in her head.

I'm angry, she says.

IX

Before she married, Moll's grandmother travelled to Dublin to pray to Saint Valentine's bones. Guide me, she begged that body. Keep me right.

Things don't make sense but she doesn't ask them to. She buys cards at the church shop, Mass cards, ones with blessings: I prayed for you at the Novena. She sends cards like that all over the place. Your loved one will be remembered in the Masses, they say. xxx Rita, she writes, keeping you all in my thoughts.

Actually, Rita believes what her mother told her, sitting as a child on a carpeted stair: this life is the Hell, and on dying there's Heaven. 'O yes,' Rita says, 'my mother was a fervent believer. She was devout.' That these are not Christian beliefs does not concern her. They are Christians because they say they're Christians; she believes her mother, does not question any priest.

Moll sees this, sometimes. Rita is furious one afternoon, seeing a panel of women on the TV discuss whether or not they should have children, what considerations there are. 'You can't do that,' Rita says. She is stood still, watching the TV. 'If I'd thought about having children, I'd never have done it.' Moll looks at her, makes a little noise. 'We'd be a while unpacking that one,' she says. Rita turns away. Moll sees it, sometimes: this lack of questions; how Rita lives.

She goes up the stairs, tells Moll she needs to take down the BLM poster she's put up her bedroom window. She brings up veggie goujons and juice, the concentrate that gets diluted; she doesn't even pretend to have a reason. Moll lies on the bed, her face to the wall. She says, 'You couldn't get the boys to poster-paint rainbows for the doctors fast enough when people were doing that.' She doesn't say, Are you embarrassed of me? They don't argue, because Rita doesn't argue. She says, 'This is not a democracy.' She takes the poster down on her way out.

There she is: sucking the marrow from the bones of a

roast chicken, putting on gold jewellery to leave the house, grabbing the head of any grandchild mid-nosebleed, pinching their nose, tilting them back. She buys hanging baskets, trailing red geraniums. She spits at a woman who knocks on the door about abortion services. She irons every item of Moll's clothing, down to individual socks. In a queue at the pharmacy, she hears someone say: 'Raise your children and you can spoil your grandchildren, spoil your children and you'll end up raising your grandchildren.' It's on her mind, then. She looks at her daughter, just in, working at the laptop, her shoulders rounded, white computer light on her corrugated forehead. She writes these cards: xxx Rita, she says. She listens to Moll talk about her geography trip: they took water samples from the river to identify the insects, but they couldn't do it: there were none there. Moll's mother comes home from work, lies flat on the sofa. Something happened with a butterfly knife. There are struggles. There are pains. All Rita says, all her daughter's life, is: 'Don't do anything stupid.' And then what can be said?

It upsets Rita, sometimes: the way things are remembered. She mentions at a dinner that she taught the children to swim and Moll's mother laughs, a small, tinselly sound. 'You pushed us in,' she says. 'You said, for god's sake, could youse not even float?' It hurts Rita, to be remembered this way. Here they are, in Rita's house. Here they sit, eating Rita's food.

You almost killed me. Yes, Rita thinks it. Every one of you—I almost died. She lost teeth in her pregnancies. They fizzed at her bones. Where was the shape of herself?—she was somewhere, had been somewhere—Moll's mother broke Rita's coccyx on her way out: her back bone. She often thinks it. You broke my fucking back. People didn't see her, then. But it's the way that it was. Things don't make sense. She doesn't ask them to. I had to do it, she thinks. Why shouldn't you?

She loves them. When they are not together, she texts them, her children, her grandchildren. *Just lit you a candle*, she texts. Or: *Said special prayer. You should feel it in couple mins.*

She texts Moll something like this: *You should feel it kick in.* Moll cannot tell if her grandmother is serious. She messages her back, says: *How will I know when it's reached me*?

Rita texts her back: *Will all feel lighter i think*.

Daisy Hill

THE DOG

John takes the animal to the vet because of its breathing, because of its shitting on the flat's pale laminate flooring, because of lumps which are new. Perhaps she needs, he concedes, an operation. The vet looks, opens the dog's mouth, palpates its skin, and says, yes: there's not long to go now. He recommends, he has to recommend, euthanasia.

No, John says.

It is the only kind response; there is nothing he can do.

No, John says. It is all he can say. He leans heavily against the vet's examination table, his mouth slightly open. The vet does not turn around. His fingers are still running over the dog's back, over the metastases. She dies peacefully, the vet says: no fear, no pain. You've got to give her her dignity.

How long does she have? John asks him. How long do we have?

That night, John calls Rowan on Facebook messenger. Before the call even connects, his skin crawls with embarrassment and he ends it. He sits with the phone in his hand, aware of his own breathing.

In the morning, the phone tells him that Rowan's messaged. It surprises John. The message from Rowan says, you free saturday? thinking of heading down

John says, Whatever suits.

Then he says, Yes cub. I'll be about

When the coach he's left the city on reaches the bus station, Rowan heads to the toilet and then emerges into the carpark with his backpack on, looking for John. There's a car beeping its horn but it doesn't occur to Rowan that it might be beeping at him, even as his phone rings: Shane Hughes is calling him on WhatsApp.

Alright, Shane? Rowan says.

Are you thick or what? says Shane. He beeps again.

Rowan feels self-conscious walking over. Shane looks distracted, even from a distance, even through the windscreen, his hands on the wheel, his eyes checking the mirrors. His car is large and white, just dirty enough that there are defined handprints on its surface.

Took your time, Shane says. John asked me to lift you. He starts driving before Rowan has his seatbelt on.

Shane is twenty-seven. He's not much older than Rowan, who's twenty-three, but Shane feels himself to be adult in ways he imagines Rowan could not even understand: Shane is married, his wife pregnant; he talks bulking and cutting, consumes kilos of protein powder, is always blending and gagging on thick, grey shakes. He works for his father, Máirtín, a builder, has done since before he left school. His phone is playing a Spotify mix called *This is Coldplay* and as they drive, Rowan notices a small pin of a Saint Brigid's cross stuck to the car's dashboard. Shane's mother, Michelle, always has bits like that in her car. She has a feather she finds, and feels to be

Daisy Hill

a sign from her parents, tucked into her sun-visor.

He softens. Here, Shane, he says. Thanks for the lift.

Shane nods. You need to get yourself a car.

Yeah. But I mean, the buses are decent.

In the city, maybe. There's nothing out here.

I do live in the city, Shane, Rowan says.

Shane's phone plays Viva La Vida.

Rowan asks about Shane's wife, a teacher who, as an extra-curricular, helps train P6s and P7s into altar-servers, and her sister, the nineteen-year-old soloist singing 'As I Kneel Before You (Ave Maria)' at Shane's wedding. Shane evidently thinks the question about his wife's sister is strange. Grand, he says. On an Erasmus year: Madrid.

He wishes he'd done it, Shane says. He wishes he'd taken a few years in Spain, in Portugal. Within minutes, he is talking about Australia and how, despite the news of people burning to death in their cars, of floods so destructive their own government calls them 'rain-bombs', it is just a better place to be. He says, twice: they've got it made over there.

You want to, then, Rowan says, you're thinking of moving?

Shane shakes his head. You'd need to do it when you're young.

Rowan doesn't know where they're going. John lives in a flat Rowan hasn't seen, the flat they buy less than a year before Zita dies. The flat's too small for everything then, and Zita's waked at Shane's father's place, just outside the town. Rowan has meant to visit. He hasn't wanted to, but he knows that he should have by now.

John makes this joke, something like, I should've seen her coming! He meets Zita at a free gig in Ormeau Park; she walks right up to him. The joke he makes is, I should've seen her coming, as though he would've moved, but John does see her coming: he watches her walk and he feels himself tense, not even wanting to hope that this woman, that she might, she could be, walking towards him.

She gets this sickness and it swamps her. When she recovers, they leave their jobs, buy a skeleton of a cottage with a flagstone floor, and she has a card stuck to the door of the kitchen cupboard, the card her corporate colleagues give her on leaving: Zita McVeigh, your life is a movie, it says. Zita loves that line.

Zita is the first person Rowan ever tells about wanting to be a writer. Every time he sees her, he doesn't but he wants to, he almost tells her about the list. On his dad's anniversary, she texts: he still seems so alive

It means a lot to Rowan.

She's sick again. Zita is compelled: she knows what she has to do. John will live in a shrine, if she does not make him move. He will keep everything, if she does not throw it out. So, even sick, this is what she does. They sell everything. They buy and move to a small flat in John's hometown. In the new place, she imagines John walking to meet friends. Yes, she can picture him taking the dog to the park, whistling home from a pint. There he is. There will be pub quizzes, she thinks. He will win. This is how it is: she sits in the hospital. The doctor begins by asking if there is somebody with her today. No, Zita says. She wants John to hear it from her. I'm so sorry, Zita, the doctor says to her. Her concern is singular: she must make her death something John can survive.

Shane pulls into a street with an apartment building on the corner. John is stood on the pavement, waiting. The car mounts the kerb in parking and as John crosses the street,

Shane lifts one finger off the steering wheel in a wave. He puts his window down as their uncle comes close to them.

I've to be off here, John, Shane says.

O, right, yea, says John.

He and Rowan stand watching as Shane drives away, the white car with all its handprints heading back up the street, and the sight of it reminds Rowan, for a second, of all those caves with the handprints in. He finds it touching, and then he finds that embarrassing. It's good to see you, John, he says, his arms feeling long by his sides.

I'm sorry I couldn't lift you myself, John says. But the car, there's something with, sure, the clutch is banjaxed.

No worries, says Rowan. It was good to see Shane. He follows John across the street, into the apartment building. How are things, anyway? he asks.

At the closed doors of the building's lift, they each wait for the other to press its small square button. It's brutal, John says. That's the truth.

O, Rowan says. He says, God, John, I'm sorry.

She's in pain all the time, John says. Rowan is startled to hear real emotion. O, you'll look at her, you'll think she's well enough, John is saying. But I look at her and I know.

Rowan presses the lift button. There's the sound of the lift moving, like bones crunching in joints.

They said they won't treat her because it won't, it just wouldn't do anything. She has painkillers, but it's not, that's not the same.

The lift comes and its doors heave open. John doesn't move. Sometimes I think, he says. Sometimes I think, when I see pictures of her, sometimes I think, when you look at anyone, if you knew what was coming, would you do it, would you want it, would you want, he says, not finishing, swaying, his body gently swaying with the movement of someone who cannot stand for long. She could, John says, I could, we, we might've just died at birth.

Rowan does not make eye contact.

He steps into the lift which has a mirror, a panel of six buttons and a phone for if the lift breaks; beside the phone is a note sellotaped to the wall, saying that the phone doesn't work and that its manufacturer has been notified. The note is dated two years previous.

You're thinking, says John, you're thinking, John, it's a dog.

No! says Rowan, too quickly.

John stands with his eyes closed, swaying. I can hear myself, he says. I can hear it. It's a dog, he says, and when he rubs the skin of his forehead, Rowan sees the dry skin of John's hands, cracked at the joints. There's fuck all wrong with the car, John says. I couldn't get you because I can't, I can't leave her. The lift moves upwards gummily, in sudden, sticky movements.

The door to John's second-floor flat is unlocked.

Inside, there is a dog lying in a bed beside a laptop, sat on the flat's grey floor, open and playing a three-hour long YouTube video of a crackling log fire.

John sees him looking. He heads to the kitchen-end of the flat's living room, to its sink and microwave oven. He lifts a kettle, struggles with a tap, says, tea?

That'd be great, John, Rowan says. He feels real relief. He sinks down onto his haunches beside the dog. It doesn't look very awful, he thinks. It has all its hair, but there are lumps on its body, lines of bulky lumps on its face sat like cheekbone augments. He reaches out to pet her but then thinks that he shouldn't: he doesn't know where she's sore. She's so big, he says. A lurcher, isn't she?

She's all kinds, says John. That's a real dog for you. All those big dogs together.

He stands at the sink. Rowan sits on the floor. The kettle boils, the water jumps, the kettle clicks off. John stands at the sink, the tanned, stretchy skin of his arms bare, his T-shirt riding up to show stomach imprinted by the tightness of a belt, the one forgotten piercing of his ear filled in like a railway tunnel. There is, Rowan sees, the absence of Zita on John's actual body, on the form of him, in the hair that is thick in his ears, at his nose, that grows unevenly with tufts, with absences, from the top of his head: Zita would be there, gently shaping him, and though he has called John by his first name for years he feels desperate to, instead, call him uncle, to put some order back on things, to see only the amount of grief that he imagines a nephew would be allowed.

There he is, his uncle John, there he is: at a sink filled with used dishes, grim mugs, a bowl overflowing with a mound of used teabags; there he is, there's the full of him, swaying, swaying.

Fuck, Rowan says.

THE FLAT

John's taken something but Rowan doesn't know what, and now he sees it he doesn't know how he ever didn't. John's telling Rowan about the Mormon woman downstairs who moved here because God compelled her. She tells me He's called her here, John says and then he laughs, a sound that comes from his mouth slowly, in chunks, and he says, that's all we need, ha-ha, Rowan, I says til her, that's all we fucking need. He is on the floor, his hand on the dog's bed. His voice is heavy falling from his mouth, sounding familiar and terrible. It has taken an hour to get the admission that something's been taken, but there's no movement on what, or how much, or where he got it.

John talks of the dog. He has asked for Rowan's help in finding videos; he says it soothes her. He says he can tell. They play for the dog: one video of a greyhound race, a compilation of cats playing with squeaking toys, and two videos of wolves howling in various national parks. The dog lies prone. She is unresponsive.

John says, Rowan, you see those pictures at the TV, bring them here. There are two frames on the TV stand. One's a photo of Zita; the other is John, Dónal, Michelle and their mother, stood outside their father's shop in Hill Street. Give them here, says John.

Rowan doesn't want to. He doesn't move.

At secondary school, when Rowan's dad dies, Rowan's Head of Year calls him into his classroom to give him a printout, a sheet of emotions arranged in a circle. Each emotion links up with more descriptive words; one emotion, such as ANGER, splinters off into: FRUSTRATION, JEALOUSY, DISAPPOINTMENT, RESENTMENT. It is important, says the man, that Rowan stays in touch with his emotions, that he really feels his feelings. The other teachers feel this is very progressive of the Year Head. He gets a lot of clout in the staff-room for it. But Rowan knows, there, in his uncle's flat, that his emotions are unknowable. It has always been true.

It happens: he is subsumed by the absence of feeling. He is overwhelmed with the absence of people.

When Rowan stands suddenly, John reaches out a hand for the photos, expectant.

I'm going to the toilet, Rowan says.

He closes the bathroom door. He takes satisfaction from the solid sound of its lock. There is no soap and no handtowel. He wets his face. He breathes on purpose. He looks at his hands carefully. His skin is unbroken.

On his way to and from, Rowan passes the open door of John's bedroom, sees powerful, dark clusters of mould in the corners and a bed so impossibly covered with clothes and stuff that it cannot be slept in, and he knows that John isn't sleeping there, and he doesn't know what to do with that, then, feels waves from which he can only pick out pain, and panic. You're not sleeping in your bed, Rowan imagines himself saying, in a world in which he is braver. John, he says, in that world, you're not an old man. There is a smell in the hall: stale, humid. The laminate floor is uneven.

Rowan's uncle is where he was left, his hand on the dog's bed, his eyes open.

Rowan looks at John as though he has never seen him before and then he says, although the saying takes effort, although the saying makes the changes real, What the fuck is wrong with your face?

And John doesn't say anything, though perhaps those open eyes widen, as Rowan looks at his face, on the floor, his breathing slow, the sloping side of his mouth, its pool of unswallowed spit.

Stand up, Rowan says. Stand up! He is screaming.

What? John says. Or he makes a sound like that, a thick,

heavy sound that might've been that word to him. You look like my dad, Rowan says, in a world in which he can say things. It's collapsed, the face, slack, and empty, and the way there's nothing on it, no expression, and you can't move it, and it's not yours, you look like my dad, like he did, when he was dead. You can't do this to me, he says, in that world. How can you do this to me?

Rowan says, lift your arms, John. You need to, get up, we have to, and he grabs John's hands and he tries to move them. O my god, Rowan says. O my god. O my god.

There is only the fear, the dread, the pain in his arms, he is shouting, stand up, stand up, why can't you, why can't, you're too heavy, John, move, please, John, he is shouting, John, John, and he thinks: people die and they die and they die and they die.

Stand, says Rowan.

But John can't do it.

I know that you know this is serious, Rowan says. But even as he says it, Rowan has to fight a wave which tells him that maybe it is not. It is the same wave which tells him that none of this is real.

This cannot be happening, the wave says. Therefore it isn't. He is overwhelmed by the sensation that he is not alive. He sits on the edge of the sofa. There is John, on the floor. People die and they die and they die and they die.

At Shane's wedding, Zita finds Rowan crying behind the grand piano in the hotel reception. She takes him to the disabled toilet and she has him take off his tie, she undoes his top button, and she stands rubbing his back while Rowan bokes and he bokes.

She says, do you know why your daddy wanted to call

you Rowan? It's because rowans are sacred. They keep evil away. She says, I'll tell you this, you won't know it: sometimes we use your name for our passwords.

Her voice is low. She has her hand on his back.

Rowan moves to where John is on the floor. I'm calling an ambulance, he says.

John starts yelling, this noise that wails up and down like a siren, running out of air and stopping, slowly gasping. Who the fuck do you think you are? he's saying, the sound of his own heart drumming in his temples, I'm going fucking nowhere, I'm going nowhere, read my lips, he yells, his mouth un-moving, nowhere, nowhere, on the floor, his eyes wide, his mouth open, his lungs desperate for air but so slow to inflate, yelling, yelling, and Rowan feels as though he's losing blood, the edge of his vision whitening, and John is desperate, desperate to stay, I won't go, I'm not moving, I'm not fucking moving, and he hits with his arms, he hits, he yells, he yells, so I'll die, he yells, let me die.

Rowan calls Shane Hughes four times. Shane doesn't say anything when the line connects, as though he's hoping Rowan's called him by accident. He makes it to the flat in twenty-three minutes.

Well, Johnny? Shane says, when he sees John on the floor.

Let me fucking die, John screams.

Shane looks at Rowan. He needs a fucking ambulance, he says.

They can't force him, says Rowan, we can't force him and I, I don't know, can they take him like this? Will they take him?

Then he goes, defensive, I don't fucking know, Shane, do I?

Shane shakes his head. Can you stand for me, John? he says, and then he shouts, over the roar of John's throat, John! John, it's Shane, this is Shane! Can you stand, mate?

He holds out his hands and Rowan says, no, he's not going to do it, and Shane looks at Rowan with something Rowan reads as dislike, as close to disgust, as John takes them, as he grasps Shane's hands. Shane pulls and John groans and Shane gets him up almost to standing. I need you to stay still for me, Shane says, as John sways, as he is already falling back. Then Shane snaps, Move back, Rowan, and he bends to do a fireman's lift. John yells the sounds that make up the dog's name, manages some of them. The animal understands well enough. When that body finally moves, it bites.

THE VENDING MACHINE

They sit in a row in Daisy Hill Hospital: Shane, Rowan, and Shane's father, Máirtín. John has been taken through double-doors, prioritised through initial triage questions. He's had something, Rowan begs, he's taken something, I don't know what.

Is he an addict? asks a member of the staff, cold. Rowan and Shane look at each other. Lads, the nurse says, does he do this often? But they don't know.

The TV in A&E is showing *Crime Stoppers*. Police want help identifying a man caught on CCTV in a supermarket in Fermanagh stealing two containers of baby formula. They show the man's face in close-up. Please contact the show with any information you may have, the presenter says.

So you contact them anonymously, is it? says Máirtín, eating. Surely people would just report people they don't like? That'd be a concern of mine.

When Michelle dies, Máirtín gets big into the cycling. He looks well now, his core and legs firm under his clothes, but there's no doubt his small-talk has suffered. He arrives just before John's taken through the double-doors. He says, when he sees him, well, Johnny! How's the form?

Boys O boys, Máirtín says, sitting down. He has sandwiches from the 24-hour petrol station. He passes Rowan a piri-piri chicken wrap. You should've rang me, kid, he says, Shane told me it was just you there. Rowan nods. He does not have Máirtín's number.

He and Shane get John down to the car, to the hospital, by walking with him in the middle, his arms round their shoulders. They carry him, his feet lifted, for some seconds, entirely off the ground. His mouth loses spit, flowing streams of it, and his open eyes widen in anger, in alarm. Let me die, he says still, though with lessening force.

Shane drives them, his bitten hand large on the steering wheel, the skin punctured in places, in others scraped where the dog's teeth do not tear flesh. It upsets John, this hand. He sees how weak the dog has become. That's what I was saying, Rowan, she can't chew, she can't swallow, John thinks, distressed. Only some of these words make it out. They get mostly a moan, something agonising, but Shane, who hears she, who hears weak, smacks his aching hand against the steering wheel, shouts, You're sorry for the fucking dog, John?

Shane's waiting, now, for a tetanus injection. He takes a call from his twenty-five-year-old wife and wanders around the waiting room, settling to lean against one of the vending machines.

The TV shows two items on how the healthcare trust in which the hospital is situated is in crisis, and emergency surgeries are unable to go ahead. Máirtín says, O, for dear's sake.

It is noisy but Rowan is not really there, not really hearing it. My dad did this thing, Rowan says, he was like, he could never tell you to do anything because if something happened it'd be his fault. Did you notice that? He and my mum talked about it, he knew he did it. He'd think, I can't tell Rowan he should go swimming, because what if he goes, and he drowns, and I'm the one who told him to go? What if I say he should go out and he gets, like, crushed in a crowd?

Máirtín has tensed. He looks straight ahead. Directly in front of him, he can see his son at the vending machine. How's that my fault? Shane is saying to his phone. I heard you, I'm saying, how's that my fault?

Things are a bit strained between them just now, Máirtin says, nodding his head in that general direction: Shane and the wife. She wants, for the pregnancy, a big party, get it presents, pick a name, all that craic, and our Shane's not having it. Shane says it's unlucky, doing all that before the baby's even born. Counting your chickens. But she's not happy. She says it's superstitious shite, that he's superstitious. Well, Máirtín says. You know our Shane. That's all Michelle. He gets all that from his mum.

Shane! Máirtín shouts suddenly. He jerks a thumb at the vending machine. Will you grab us a packet of Prawn Cocktail?

Shane holds up a hand. The hand says: whisht.

I read this poem, Rowan says. It's called 'No Explosions', by Naomi Shihab Nye. It goes: 'To enjoy/fireworks/you would have/to have lived/a different kind/of life.'

Máirtín says, eventually: You wrote that?

No, no, says Rowan. I didn't write it.

You do that, though, isn't it? Books and that?

Yeah. I mean, I try sometimes. I do try to write stuff.

He closes his eyes. I just, when I read it, I thought of you all. There's all these little things you say. There's so much that was normal.

Your dad, Máirtín says awkwardly, Rowan, you know I knew Dónal since I was, what, fourteen? He breathes out hard through his nose. He raises his hands. We were, Christ, we were always, it, it's terrible, everything that's happened, don't think I don't, that I don't think that. But I believe, these things, they're the making of us. It'll be the making of you. Some day, you'll look back and it'll all make sense. Sure, just look at our Shane.

Rowan thinks to point out that there is but four years between himself and Shane.

He doesn't.

It'll all come together, says Máirtín.

I appreciate that, Rowan says.

Your dad was my best man, says Máirtín. O my god, his speech. I'll never forget it. He brought the house down. You've never heard the like. He said, he said, O dear god, he said—

There's a pause then. It yawns, stretches, becomes a pause so long that Rowan knows Máirtín will not speak again.

It's okay, Rowan says, into the hum of the waiting room.

Máirtín clears his throat. It's on a tape somewhere.

When John comes back into the waiting area, a doctor comes with him. He has to be admitted, the doctor says, but there's no bed. They've ruled out haemorrhage, but we are, you have to understand, says the doctor, we are just so busy. You are our priority, she says, but it's going to be a long time. She'll be back with news when she has it.

Led to them, John sits heavily on a seat and his legs splay, as though lacking muscle tone enough to keep them together. His head seems too heavy for his neck. It lolls. John, shouts Máirtín, and he receives the guts of a thumbs-up.

Shane comes back from the vending machine, phone in his pocket.

Here, says Máirtín, slapping his knees. I may head on here. He stands, his coat folded over his arm. His face is so bare that Rowan wonders if he's shaving as Shane calls him, just as he's coming out. Don't be a stranger, he says to Rowan, pulling him from a handshake up into a hug which is cool, which is brief, efficient.

Drop us a text anytime, he says.

He has not given Rowan his number.

Máirtín says, alright, John? to the head, slumped.

John lifts a hand.

You'll be grand, says Máirtín.

No, says John.

You'll be grand! says Máirtín, louder.

In another hour, a doctor calls Shane for his tetanus shot.

Rowan sits beside John, half-watching the TV. He cannot sit comfortably. I'm sorry, John says, though Rowan doesn't understand the noises, I told you I'm sorry.

When he checks his phone Rowan has a text from his mother, Deirdre. He rings, and she answers, and it helps immediately. At the sound of her voice, Rowan can see her blonde highlights, picture her sitting in the rocking-chair she bought at Habitat For Humanity, sanded and coated with a spray-can of paint, can see her nails, smooth and pale, the river basins round her eyes. He tells her that John collapsed, because he has to put words on it and John is still sat beside him. He says that they're at the hospital.

O, John's been having a hard time, his mother says, and when she says it, Rowan remembers that it's true. She asks to speak to him, and Rowan holds the phone to John's ear. He hears some of what his mother says to John, about eating, about sleeping. John does neither.

You're sad, says Rowan's mother.

O God, Deirdre, John slurs. It's sad. It's sad.

John is admitted. They find a bed for him in a corridor. A bed's a bed, a nurse says.

They attempt to hug him before he goes. They seize his shoulders. His arms are weak, dead-weight. His eyes are wide. Mum's going to come see you tomorrow, Rowan says. She told me on the phone there. John, I'm talking about Deirdre, he says. Deirdre'll be down to see you tomorrow.

Good luck, says Shane. Alright, mate, good luck.

Rowan sits down again once John is through the double-doors. Shane stays standing. Look, I've got to be getting home, he says. But I can run you to the bus station. I don't know when the next bus is but you'll be alright hanging round, won't you, you can just wait there?

Yeah, says Rowan. Thanks, he says.

It is dark and the car is cold. The journey feels exhausting, even as it will take only minutes, even as they are only seconds in. There is a sense between them, now, of something shared, but there is, still, everything, everything sat in the silence, and Rowan, watching the black road ahead of them light up and light up and light up with Shane's headlights, can hear, he still hears, the yelling, still feels the ringing of it, remembers every word, every roar, could write it all out; he can see every face he watched in the hospital, can see John on the floor, feel the weight of him, the unbearable weight of him on his shoulders, on his back.

He watches Shane's hand, tattooed with the dying dog's teeth, turn and turn and turn the steering wheel and he thinks: people die and they die and they die and they die. He says to Shane that he should have known there was something wrong immediately. He should have known from John's voice and from the swaying and from what he said in the morning, from the way that he said it, he should've known he was fucked, and he should've called sooner and he's sorry, it's his fault, he should have gotten them to the hospital, he should've known when John wanted the photo of him and the others from before their dad was taken. As he says it, his mouth fills with spit, the warm thin spit that rises up before vomit and he says, he's the only one of them left.

There is a pause.

Shane's air freshener swings.

You need to get back into the driving, Shane says. I'm not saying it's easy, but it all clicks one day. It comes. One day, you just know.

It's awkward, then.

Rowan sits with his hands clasped, wipes them on his knees. Do you never think about how they all get sick? he says.

Shane stares ahead. It's different things, he says.

No, it's not.

Shane doesn't say anything. He overtakes on a bend.

It's bad luck, he says. I looked into it, with mum. But she didn't even have any of the risk factors. She didn't smoke often, she didn't drink too much, she didn't have a stressful life—

Are you taking the piss, Shane? Rowan says, his surprise honest. How can you say they didn't have stressful lives?

Fuck off, says Shane. You know what I mean.

You don't think there's any connection?

I'm sick of this, right, Rowan? I'm sick of it. I don't want to talk about this. I don't want to talk to you, I'm sick of it, right? You weren't there, you remember fuck all, you just, you've got this obsession with history.

How the fuck is it history?

What do you want, Rowan? It happened, right? It happened, two sides, either side, both, it happened, it stopped.

I hate that, says Rowan. It's not both sides, it's not either side, it's this huge fucking army, it's this huge fucking state, this government that does whatever it wants, that just, that, they can kill us, and kill us.

I don't know why you're like this, I swear I don't. It's politics. It's history.

But it's my life. Rowan's hands are sweating, his hands are wet, and he's turned to Shane but Shane's not looking: he has his eyes locked on the road, his hands turning and turning, his fury a phenomenon he won't even admit.

Not that I even give a shit, alright, kid, because I fucking don't, Shane says, his head un-moving, but you've got to learn that in this life, sometimes shit just happens, right? It's not this big conspiracy. I don't know what the fuck to say to you, mate, your head's scrambled and I've been fucking saying it, don't think I've not been saying it, I've known it, mate, I can fucking see it.

It's happened your mum, Shane, says Rowan, it's happened your mum, and my dad, and then Shane is screaming, his own anger startling him: She was my mum, mine! You think you're so fucking smart? You think you know everything? Well, you can't have known her because she was my mum and she didn't care about this stuff! Are you listening to me, Rowan? She did not care! She moved the fuck on! And Dónal, okay, your dad, he was fucked up, he was a fucking headcase, but that's, that's just, he should've, he could've just caught a fucking grip.

How do you not know what it did to them? Rowan says, screaming, the sensation falling on him all at once: O my god, he thinks, he doesn't know.

Shane pulls the car over violently.

He stops it with the handbrake so that everyone and everything jolts, begins a sharp, lethal turning. The air freshener slices through close, thick air.

He says: The dog. We have to go back.

THE EXHIBITION

Gearóid Mac Lochlainn writes about, as a child, being searched by British soldiers.

Thug sé cic beag do mo shála/le mo chosa a oscailt níos leithne/mhothaigh mé méar i mo dhroim/nó b'fhéidir a ghunna. A little kick on the heels/splayed my legs/I felt a thumb, or his gun/muzzle my back.

Mhothaigh mé lámha garbha/ag cuimilt mo choirp/méara gasta ag priocadh i mo stocaí/ransú lámh i mo phócaí/bosa strainséartha/ag dul suas mo bhríste. I felt hard hands/rub my body. Hands rifled my pockets/fists knuckling in.

Ba mhian liom éalú ó na lámha seo/ar mo chorpsa/dá dtiocfadh liom rith chun an bhaile/dá dtiocfadh liom arís a bheith i mo ghasúr scoile. I wanted to escape from those hands/on my body/if I could run home/if I could just be a schoolboy again.

I needed to disappear, he writes. Nobody said it would be like this. An chéad uair a mhothaigh mé/snáthaid ghéar náire. The first time I felt/a sharp needle of shame.

Rowan's father is Dónal. He never tells his son anything specific. His are emotions that are quiet, unprocessed. He watches boxing. He loves *Riverdance*. He self-harms in ways that do not scar. When Rowan is a baby, Dónal calls him Gums. Their photo albums are largely filled with pictures of Dónal and Rowan asleep together: arms back, mouths open.

Rowan starts asking his parents things as a teenager. He reads about, he is upset by, he is angry, he says, there's this branch of the British Army called the Military Reaction Force and they've gone round Belfast in plain clothes and unmarked cars targeting civilians. One member calls the unit a 'legalised death squad'. One member says the unit's role was 'repression through fear, terror and violence'.

Dónal can't handle it. He's always going: I know! I know it! I lived it, Rowan!

He's yelling: You can't tell me anything I don't know!

He says it, you can't tell me anything I don't know, even about things he doesn't know, things he can't know, things that have only come out in recent years, because he means: there's nothing you can say that will surprise me. He means: stop telling me things.

Dónal never tells his son anything specific about what he saw. It's an impulse Rowan only understands once his dad is dead. Things hurt and they cannot be explained. What would you know of it, anyway? You weren't there.

Dónal tells Michelle about going with Rowan to the Ulster Museum, about the way that Rowan stands gawping at the Troubles' exhibition, about how he takes pictures of pictures with his phone. It feels, Dónal says to Michelle, like he has immigrated somewhere. He tries but sometimes, he's looking round, he doesn't know where he is.

At Dónal's wake, Máirtín says, sure, isn't it just like Dónal to sit there in the middle, listening to everyone and not getting involved? People laugh at this. They love Dónal.

There's this way men live, Rowan writes, with bloodshotredeyedgrief.

He is born. There is this gap: one generation. He has a list. Nothing is obvious. Nothing is explained. He hears Michelle talking, once, about a movement for civil rights: what started it all. He tells Dónal, and Dónal looks at him. He looks and looks.

He tries to write. Dónal says, too many books start with the quotes of other people. You go to read this lad's book, there's someone else there. You're thinking, who's your one? For God's sake, didn't I come here to listen to you?

He has a list. Omygod. He has his list. What they say about us—backward, sectarian, ugly, violent—is never said about them and, yet, his list: this is the British state. Waterboarding, raping, torturing innocents—British soldiers dressed in plain clothes driving round shooting civilians—this is the news, wherein we hear what they say about us: British soldier veterans are having their lives ruined by 'vexatious claims'—O it's stressful for the soldiers, they are feeling 'harassed'—they have tortured us, they have murdered us, they are the victims yet. They are people, says the news, these soldiers are people; but not their victims. He has a list. He has a page of emotions that spiral out and out. He tries to write, but he's only writing this, again and over: I would care if this were done to you.

He tries to write. At a peaceful protest of unarmed civilians against the Army's detainment, without evidence and without charge, of hundreds in internment camps, British soldiers shoot twenty-six people, murder fourteen people, almost half of whom are children, shoot unarmed civilians as they run, as they hide, as they try to help the others wounded and dying. These civilians are wounded with shrapnel, shot by soldiers with rubber bullets, beaten by soldiers with batons, run over by soldiers in Army vehicles. This is the news: the British soldiers who murdered these people will not stand trial. A British politician defends one of them on the TV, says these soldiers 'deserve' to live the rest of their lives 'in peace'.

This is the news: the British-appointed secretary for Northern Ireland says that the British military and police who carried out killings in the north were 'fulfilling their duties in a dignified and appropriate way'. They kill with impunity. This is the British state. They show a riot on the news, on the TV—this place is sectarian, backward, violent, says the TV, this is the north of Ireland: we do not know why it is the way that it is—the British state kills and it kills and it kills and it kills—he's only writing, over and over: where is it all supposed to go?

At secondary school, in the assemblies, Rowan's Head of Year talks about moving-on. The other teachers feel this is very progressive of the Year Head. He gets a lot of clout in the staff-room for it. Anyone in this place could put together anyone's atrocities, says the teacher, but, really, to what benefit?

Rowan finds a note Dónal's kept in his desk drawer, part of a note Rowan's mother wrote Dónal on the pad of post-its that used to live by the landline phone: I wish this were a world you could live in.

At the wake, Shane comes over to Rowan. He's had a drink, though the wake is dry. He says, I need to tell you something. He says, I mind Uncle Dónal, this one day, he's at the house, we're walking, he starts talking about daisies. He says there's this story about how the first one appeared when a baby died and that's why they're the colour they are, white and pink, like that baby's skin, and he says he liked it as a kid, that story, but as an adult, it's so often in his head?

Shane has Rowan by the shoulder. He looks in his face. I didn't know what to say, he says. Rowan registers the expression: he feels guilty. He feels ashamed. Maybe he thinks he could have made a difference. I remember Dónal says to me, look at them, Shane, there's millions. You can't not see them now, all those kids, everywhere.

This is the list: British soldiers murder civilians in an attack the pathologist calls 'frenzied'. They hold down and stab twenty-three-year-old civilian Andrew Murray at least thirteen times. They hold down and stab thirty-one-year-old civilian Michael Naan at least seventeen times through the heart and the chest. This is agony. This is savage, unfathomable murder. These are innocents slaughtered by the British state. Terror. But, listen, this is the news: British politicians call British soldiers the 'victims of persecution'.

Rowan hears a man, stood round his dad's coffin, saying: and sure, isn't Dónal always taking things to heart, never forgave himself that, at their mother's funeral, the priest forgot her name.

The British Army, Rowan reads, maintains that it was always, and remains, a neutral force.

There's Máirtín, leaning forward where he sits, hands clasped together between his knees. He has the head bowed, doesn't see Rowan, has the head bowed, unseeing, uneven breathing.

Our taxes pay for their guns, their boots, their salaries, their pensions, fifty million files sealed until all of us are dead, you permit it until nothing is, itself, impermissible.

Rowan says to Dónal, when Dónal is living, Why don't you tell me about this? Don't you know what they did?

He's boking in the bathroom at Shane's wedding and Zita has her hand, her warm hand, on his back. She says, Do you know why your daddy wanted to call you that, Rowan? It's because rowans are sacred. They keep evil away. She says, I'll tell you this, you won't know it: he used to love all that folklore. I remember him talking. He did all these things to keep us safe. She rubs his back and her hand makes a sound on the fabric. Maybe you didn't hear him talk so much about that, she says. As he got older, I think he got sadder about all of it lost.

I would care if this were done to you.

Boys O boys, says Máirtín. Boys O boys.

THE TRUTH

James Wray is twenty-two. He has been shot, and he is paralysed, and he is on the ground, bleeding. A British soldier approaches. He shoots James in the back at point-blank range.

*

Michael Kelly, John Young, William Nash, and Michael McDaid are seventeen, seventeen, nineteen, twenty. Michael Kelly dies in minutes. John is shot in the head. William is shot in the chest. Michael McDaid is shot in the face. They are killed by British soldiers. The British Army calls these boys gunmen, but they're not. They are civilians, and they are unarmed. William's father can see his son's face clearly. He runs to him. British soldiers shoot at him. He is shot in the arm and hit in the ribs. He drops down beside his son. He puts his hand on his son's back and says his name. Willie, he says. The boy's eyes are wide open but he is dead.

*

Jack Duddy is running. Hugh Gilmour is running. Kevin McElhinny is on his stomach, crawling. They are unarmed civilians. They are just boys, seventeen. They are killed by British soldiers who shoot them in the back and in the back and in the back.

*

Daniel Hegarty loves animals. He has the house full of stray dogs and frogs he's brought home. He is a child who hangs miraculous medals and who says, no bullets will get this house. He and his cousins have their backs to the British soldier when the soldier starts shooting. The soldier shoots Daniel's cousin, Christopher. The soldier kills Daniel: he shoots the child twice in the head. The British government calls the murdered child a terrorist.

*

John McKerr is a carpenter. He's at work in a chapel. He steps outside as the funeral of a local child begins. He is shot in the head. Local people gather. British soldiers threaten them. A woman named Maureen Heath cradles John's head in her arms. When an ambulance arrives, the soldiers refuse to allow paramedics to take him. A British soldier aims his gun at Maureen, where she sits with John, and threatens to shoot her. Go ahead and shoot, she says. John McKerr is finally taken to hospital. His family isn't informed, and they find out about his shooting in the news. He dies from his injuries after nine days. Before she passes away, Maureen Heath, the woman who held his head in her hands, talks about that moment when the British soldier threatened to shoot her. My life wasn't worth much, she says. They'd shot our priest, so what was my life worth?

*

As teenagers, James Brown and Gary English are crushed to death when British soldiers drive their Army Land Rovers into a crowd of civilians. Daniel McCooey is beaten so badly by a foot patrol of British soldiers that he dies, aged twenty. Eamon McDevitt is disabled, deaf and non-verbal. He is waving his hands; this is how he communicates. British soldiers shoot him dead.

*

Daniel Teggart is walking back from his brother's house. He's a civilian, unarmed. British soldiers shoot him fourteen times. They shoot him even when he's on the ground, even when he's dead.

*

Peter McBride is eighteen. He's walking near his home when he's stopped and searched by British soldiers. The soldiers find that Peter, a civilian, is completely unarmed. Then they shoot him in the back.

*

For no reason and without warning, British soldiers enter Patrick McElhone's family farm and shoot him through the heart. Patrick is twenty-four. He is a civilian. He is unarmed. His brother sees the soldiers who murdered his brother cheer and celebrate.

*

British soldiers kill a child named Stephen Geddis when he is ten years old. They shoot him in the head. British soldiers kill a child named Brian Stewart. They shoot him in the face. British soldiers kill a seventy-six-year-old widow named Elizabeth McGregor, shooting her in the head and body as she walks home. British soldiers kill a child named John Mooney. British soldiers kill a child named Stephen McConomy. British soldiers kill a child named Leo McGuigan. British soldiers kill a child named Danny Barrett as he sits in his own front garden. Francis McGuigan dies at twenty-three months old after British soldiers fire CS gas into his home and he breathes it in.

*

This is the Falls Road curfew. The British Army announces an indefinite curfew in one part of the city. They fly helicopters low over the houses and yell it through loudspeakers. They designate a curfew zone. They start to seal it off with barbed wire: around three-thousand tiny homes, narrow backstreets. Thousands of soldiers move into the area. They have helicopters and British Army armoured vehicles. They arrest journalists. They arrest local MP Paddy Devlin. They threaten to shoot him. They begin a search. They loot the houses. They rip up the floors, tear down the ceilings, destroy furniture. They attack civilians. They shoot. They fire 1,600 canisters of CS gas. They use catapults. The choking gas is everywhere. They raid the same houses again and again. It only ends, after two days, when women and children walk, with food and groceries, from another area, from Andersonstown, to British lines. They try to resist but in the end, soldiers have to let the crowd through. British soldiers shoot sixty-three unarmed civilians in two days. They kill four. Zbigniew Uglik is killed by a British Army sniper. British soldiers brutalise his body, kicking him, cursing him. He is twenty-three years old. Charles O'Neill is killed by the British Army. He's just home after years in England; he has his RAF card on him. British soldiers run him over. Identifying his body, Charles' family are handed his clothes in a paper bag. His RAF card is never returned. William Burns is standing at his own front door. A British soldier shoots him in the chest. Patrick Elliman is sixty-two, in his pyjamas. A British soldier shoots him in the head. When an ambulance comes, to take him the two-minute drive to the hospital, soldiers insist on searching and re-routing it. The journey then takes thirty minutes. Patrick dies. The night they shoot him, soldiers break into Patrick's home. The British Minister of State, Robert Lindsay, Lord Balniel, says he is 'deeply impressed' by the 'impartial way' the soldiers are carrying out an 'extremely difficult task'.

*

Martin Corr and another child are lifted by the British Army and taken to their barracks. Twelve years old, questioned and beaten, Martin makes it home, but he dies in his bed.

*

Aidan McAnespie is killed by the British Army. He is an unarmed civilian. He is twenty-four. Thomas Reilly is killed by the British Army. He is an unarmed civilian. He is twenty-two. Martin Malone is killed by the British Army. He is an unarmed civilian. He is eighteen.

*

Harry Duffy whistles walking home. His daughter says she can always hear him coming. Harry is grieving his late wife, raising their children. He goes out looking for his eleven-year-old daughter, who's late getting home. He is a civilian, unarmed. A British soldier shoots him in the head.

*

This is the truth: the man in charge of British soldiers in Belfast is called Frank Kitson. Two weeks after Bloody Sunday, Frank Kitson is knighted by Queen Elizabeth II for 'gallant and distinguished services' in Northern Ireland.

*

Billy McGreanery is an unarmed civilian. He is killed by a British soldier. Angela D'Arcy is an unarmed civilian. She is killed by a British soldier. Patrick McVeigh is an unarmed civilian. He is killed by British soldiers in plain-clothes who say: 'We were there to act like a terror group.' Annette

McGavigan is killed by a British soldier who shoots her in the head. The British Army reports that it has shot a gunman, but Annette is an unarmed child, killed in her school uniform. British soldiers kill Majella O'Hare. They shoot the twelve-year-old child in the back with a machine-gun. British soldiers kill a child named Carol Ann Kelly in front of her brother and friends. At her inquest, a year later, the soldiers blow kisses and jeer at the murdered child's sisters. When Carol Ann's family object, the judge threatens to hold them, the victim's family, in contempt of court. British soldiers kill Leo Norney and say he's a gunman, but Leo is a child, and he is unarmed. British soldiers kill twelve-year-old Kevin Heatley. I remember that my mother had to borrow money to pay for Kevin's funeral, his brother says. One year later, their father is found, having died by suicide.

*

The British Government's Northern Ireland Secretary says the British military and police were 'fulfilling their duties in a dignified and appropriate way'. The British Government announces an end to the 'persecution' of British soldiers. The British Queen delivers a speech outlining policies to 'tackle vexatious claims that undermine our Armed Forces'. British soldiers are to be granted immunity from prosecution for what they did in Northern Ireland.

*

In one night, the British Army kills three children, a priest, and an unarmed civilian trying to reach the injured. The British Army reports that it has shot six gunmen. One of the children is Margaret Gargan. She's murdered while talking to friends. She has a twin sister, and a younger brother, and her brother remembers, after his sister's murder, throwing a stone at a British Army Saracen. The soldiers lift him, throw him in the back, and beat him. They call him Irish scum. They kick him, slap him, and dump him in a different area, one where they know he won't be safe. They yell, Here's a Taig. The boy is horrifically beaten again, only just managing to escape. He is twelve.

*

Seamus Duffy is killed by a plastic bullet that crushes his heart and lacerates his lung. The police say they shot a petrol-bomber. Seamus's sister says that at the hospital, the police threaten her father, pushing him up against the wall and saying, keep it up and you'll be the same as your son. The police and the army harass his family for years. They stop Seamus's ten-year-old sister, asking: Is Seamus not coming out to play?

*

Liam Holden is nineteen when he is arrested, waterboarded and tortured by British soldiers into confessing to a crime that he did not commit. He is sentenced to hang. He is imprisoned for seventeen years. The torture's real, he says, in an interview. I'm real.

*

Dessie Healey is killed by the British Army. He is fourteen. His friend, Martin, is there. Martin's family are burnt out of their home as children. They're rehoused. British soldiers raid the house constantly. They're always coming in, coming up the stairs. Her whole life, Martin's little sister Julie is terrified of the soldiers. When she's fourteen, they kill her, too.

*

Daisy Hill

At their party conference, the British Prime Minister complains about activist, left-wing human rights lawyers going after the bravest of the brave, promising to defend British soldiers from people's 'vexatious claims'. On the news, British politicians talk about ending 'the relentless pursuit of those who served their country in Northern Ireland'.

*

Where is it all supposed to go?

*

Billy McKavanagh is twenty-one. He, his brother, Patrick, and his cousin, Teddy, are walking near their home. When they see British soldiers, they run. The soldiers kill Billy. They shoot him in the back, through the shoulder-blades, from close range. His brother and cousin sit with his cooling body. An armoured Army vehicle arrives. Billy's brother and cousin are taken in the back and tortured, attacked with rifle-butts, clubbed with guns, hooded, beaten with batons. One soldier says that he saw Patrick and Teddy just after Billy had been murdered and that, on seeing them again, when the soldiers finally bring them to the police station, Billy's brother and cousin are so horrifically injured that he could not have recognised them had they not been identified to him.

*

British soldiers are having their lives ruined, says the news.

*

Bobby Clarke is an unarmed civilian. He is helping families with children move to safety. He has just taken a child to a nearby street, where they can shelter, and he is crossing an area of wasteground as he walks back. British soldiers shoot him in the back. The bullet exits across his spine.

*

Father Hugh Mullan sees Bobby shot. He is an unarmed civilian. As he moves, he waves a white cloth. He goes to Bobby, waving this white cloth, and gives him Last Rites. British soldiers shoot the priest in the back. He dies moaning.

*

Francis Quinn sees British soldiers shoot the priest. Distraught, he goes to help. An unarmed civilian, he is nineteen years old. British soldiers shoot him in the head.

*

Noel Phillips is nineteen years old. He has just finished work. British soldiers shoot him. On the ground, wounded, he cries out for help and Joan Connolly, a mother of eight, hears him. She says, it's alright, son, I'm coming to you. Many witnesses repeat this. It's alright, son, I'm coming to you. British soldiers shoot Joan Connolly in the face. She doesn't die for hours. Later, witnesses see a British soldier exit a British Army vehicle and approach nineteen-year-old Noel Phillips, where he lies, wounded. The soldier executes the teenager, shooting him behind each ear with a shotgun.

*

They leave Joan Connolly where she lies beside Noel's body. Joan has eight children, her youngest aged two. Her daughter says that Joan used to make the British soldiers sandwiches. She says that Joan used to say, God help them, they are someone's son. Joan bleeds to death in a field. Three British soldiers admit shooting her. This is the truth: nobody is ever charged.

ACKNOWLEDGEMENTS

All of those named in the final section of the final story, 'Daisy Hill', are real people killed by British state forces.

I would like to acknowledge works which have informed my own understanding—in particular the work of Gearóid Mac Lochlainn, United Campaign Against Plastic Bullets, Relatives For Justice, Ballymurphy Massacre Group, The Museum of Free Derry, and the book, *Children of the Troubles*—and I need to acknowledge the men, women and children I named, as well as all of those I couldn't. They will be remembered.

For myself, I'm grateful to Thomas Morris, Tracy Bohan, Declan Meade and Danny Denton.

Caithfidh mé buíochas a thabhairt do mo ghrá geal, do mo dheartháireacha is do mo thuistí:

> *Siúd ar mo mháthair*
> *a thóg mé ar a brollach*
> *agus le m'athair*
> *a thóg mé le saothar a chnámha.*

Keep in touch with Granta Books:

Visit granta.com to discover more.

GRANTA